STOLEN CARS

MYSTERY, CRIME, AND MAHEM
ISSUE 18

LEAH R CUTTER   JOSLYN CHASE   CHRIS CHAN
DIANA DEVERELL   ROBERT JESCHONEK
ANNIE REED   DAVID H. HENDRICKSON
KARI KILGORE   LIBBY FISCHER HELLMANN
MICHELE LANG   CATE MARTIN

KNOTTED ROAD PRESS

Stolen Cars
Mystery, Crime, and Mayhem: Issue 18
Copyright © 2024
All rights reserved

Published 2024 by Knotted Road Press
www.KnottedRoadPress.com

Cover art:
car-drift-drifting-car-racing-5500794 © ahghost53 | Pixabay

Cover and Interior design copyright © 2024 Knotted Road Press
www.KnottedRoadPress.com

Never miss an issue of Mystery, Crime, and Mayhem! Get yourself a subscription!

https://www.mysterycrimeandmayhem.com/product/mcm-subscription/

This book is licensed for your personal enjoyment only. All rights reserved. This is a work of fiction. All characters and events portrayed in this book are fictional, and any resemblance to real people or incidents is purely coincidental.
No part of this book may be reproduced in any form or by any electronic or mechanical means, including information storage and retrieval systems, without written permission from the author, except for the use of brief quotations in a book review.

Essay: The Agatha Christie Serial Killer © 2024 by Chris Chan

The Joyride © 2024 by Leah R Cutter

Cool Ride © 2024 by Diana Deverell

The Vanishing Convertible © 2024 by Cate Martin

Dumber Than Dirt © 2024 by Libby Fischer Hellmann

Taking Care of Each Other In Our Own Way © 2024 by Kari Kilgore

Pay Up Or Walk To School © 2024 by Chris Chan

Always Gonna Happen © 2024 by Joslyn Chase

Saturday Night Special © 2024 by Michele Lang

Dodging Bullets © 2024 by David H. Hendrickson

The Zombie Rideshare © 2024 by Robert Jeschonek

Be Someone © 2024 by Annie Reed

INTRODUCTION

LEAH R CUTTER

Many years ago I came across this fascinating news article. If I'm remembering correctly, a person died, and a few years later, their storage space rent was due. The owners of the storage space went into the building and then called the police.

Seemed the place was full of cars.

Stolen cars.

They weren't all new cars. Some of the cars had been stolen decades before. They were well taken care of. All of them ran. They had more miles on them than when they'd been stolen, but not too many.

Seemed that the thief had occasionally driven the cars, but mostly, just kept them to look at.

One guy, who'd had his convertible stolen

back in the 1960s, was finally able to get it back. Surprised the heck out of him. Particularly since it was still in mint condition.

I've always wanted to do an anthology about stolen cars. In fact, that was the general idea behind the *Stolen* anthology that I did.

The stories in this anthology delighted me. I feel as though this is a really strong issue of MCM. (Then again, I almost always feel that way!)

One of the things I hadn't expected was how often the story wasn't about the stolen car, but what that car represented.

It's often said, particularly in the US, that you are what you drive. What was stolen wasn't just about the vehicle, but what that act of stealing meant, and how to make things right.

Crime stories are all about bringing order to chaos, even when that chaos is certain to keep going to continue repeating, as is mentioned in more than one of these stories as well.

So strap yourself in for another fun ride.

Leah R Cutter
April 2024

ESSAY: THE AGATHA CHRISTIE SERIAL KILLER

CHRIS CHAN

Fans of crime fiction and television may be familiar with this plotline: a mystery writer is drawn into an actual homicide case when a crime is based on one of the author's own novels. This was the premise of "Flowers for Your Grave," the pilot episode of the television series *Castle*. At the start of that series, crime writer Richard Castle (Nathan Fillion) was drawn into an actual NYPD investigation when a serial killer began arranging his own victims' crime scenes into tableaus replicated from Castle's novels. Castle's involvement led to an eight-season partnership assisting the NYPD with solving homicides.

Similarly, on *Murder, She Wrote*, killers sometimes borrowed ideas from Jessica Fletcher's crime novels, such as transferring an innocent person's fingerprints from a glass onto another, potentially incriminating surface with the help of a strip of cellophane tape. Bestselling author Jeffrey Deaver's short story "Copycat" is based on a comparable plotline: a brutal pair of killings mirrors a talented novelist's book, and the police have to find out who ripped off the author's fictional crime.

The aphorism "life imitates art" is universally known in part because it is true. In real life, sometimes crimes are inspired by fiction. Killers and attempted murderers in Canada, Norway, Sweden, the United Kingdom, and the United States have all claimed to have been motivated to take lives based on how well they related to the titular character of the television series *Dexter* (though none of these actual criminals followed the fictional serial killer's code of only harming guilty murderers).

Other individuals have committed vicious crimes based on horror movies, such as *A Nightmare on Elm Street*, *Scream*, *Halloween*, and *Saw*. But not all criminals who plagiarize their ideas turn to violent, gory movies. One serial killer was inspired by an author known for creating fictional crimes set in British manor houses and close-knit English villages, as well as exotic locales, often in the Middle East.

It's not surprising that a real-life serial killer would have been aware of the world's bestselling mystery writer. Agatha Christie's books have been a phenomenon since she first started publishing mystery novels in the early 1920's. Christie's writing career went far longer than most of her compatriots in what was termed "The Golden Age of British Crime Fiction," and before she died in 1976, she wrote sixty-six mystery novels, scores of short stories, several plays, two memoirs, and numerous poems, including many works that were published posthumously.

Christie's mysteries have sold so many copies that only the Bible and the works of William Shakespeare have surpassed her sales totals. Her works have been translated into over a hundred languages, and nearly all of her mysteries have been adapted for the screen, in some cases seven times or more. Every country in the world is filled with fans who enjoy her books.

And in 2009, there was a woman in Iran who used Christie's mysteries as part of a string of serial killings.

Iran is home to many enthusiastic readers of Christie's work. Christie travelled throughout the Middle East with her archaeologist husband Max Mallowan, and some of their trips took her to Iran. Christie often turned her travel destinations into settings in her mysteries. The short story "The Gate of Shiraz" is set in Iran. The story features the retired civil servant Parker Pyne, who specializes in bringing happiness to unfulfilled people. Pyne's transcontinental vacation, told over a series of six short stories, take him aboard the Orient Express, on a cruise of the Nile (Christie's more famous detective, Hercule Poirot, would also solve crimes in these locales), and to Syria,

Iraq, Jordan, and Greece. Along the way, Pyne solves a pair of murders, resolves a blackmailing attempt, foils a kidnapping, and recovers a stolen jewel. "The Gate of Shiraz" is a mystery about the mysterious death of a young woman, and the noblewoman who withdrew into seclusion after her companion died. When this story was published in the 1930's, Great Britain had economic and political dominance over Iran, though the region was not technically a colonized part of the British Empire. Due to Britain's influence over Iran, resentment against the United Kingdom is common amongst many segments of the Iranian population today. However, these strong emotions towards the English have not tarnished Christie's popularity amongst Iranians.

More than thirty years after Christie's death, one of her Iranian readers used what she learned from Christie's books in a way that would definitely have met with Christie's disapproval.

In May 2009, a handful of Western news sources released articles about a young woman known as Mahin, who allegedly took the lives of at least six people before being captured. It was not until months later that her full name, Mahin Qadri (also spelled Qadiri or Ghadiri in some reports), was released to the West. The news reports trumpeted that Mahin was Iran's first female serial killer.

The crimes took place between February 2008 and May 2009 in Qazvin, a city in northwestern Iran, a little bit south of the Caspian Sea and around sixty miles from Tehran. The killings take on an added layer of mystery because the English-language newspaper reports consistently contradicted each other on the details of the case. Some reports announced that body count was no higher than four, others said five, whereas other articles stated that the total number of slayings was six. Some of this confusion stems from the fact that two deaths were not attributed to Mahin for some time after the initial arrest. Mahin's total number of victims was six– at least, six known victims. Some newspaper articles attributed the causes of death to smothering, while others insisted that the victims died of strangling. Due to the conflicting news reports, the precise details of the crimes are shrouded in an aura of uncertainty.

Just like the factual aspects of the case, the psychological aspects of Mahin's violent psyche cannot be determined with any degree of accuracy based on the journalistic accounts of her crimes. The paltry references to her mental state are provided by quotes from Iranian law enforcement officials, which means that any insights into her mind are filtered through the public utterances of the officials trying to convict her. Mahin is never quoted directly, and the entirety of the news coverage of her crimes only contains a few brief sentences attempting to describe her mental state. Mahin's character is a bigger mystery than her crimes, which were fairly easy to unravel once a murder she attempted to commit went awry, leading to her capture.

On May 11th, 2009, a sixty-year-old woman frantically sought help on the streets of Qazvin, claiming that a young woman had tried to kill her. This unnamed almost-victim explained that the suspect had offered her a ride home from religious services, but the seemingly friendly young woman's behavior had set off some red flags, so the sexagenarian had managed to escape from the car unharmed, and soon managed to find the police.

The police quickly accepted the woman's story. Over the past year, four women in their fifties and sixties had been found dead in isolated areas of Qazvin. Their jewelry and other valuables had been stolen. The causes of death were either smothering or strangulation, depending on the conflicting news reports on the case. Prior to their deaths, each of the women had been heavily drugged and rendered unconscious. In one case, a woman had apparently recovered from her anesthetic-induced stupor, and was fatally bludgeoned with a piece of iron. The police had no suspects, but there was one clue that made the authorities wonder if a female was involved in the crimes– a woman's footprint was discovered close to one of the murder victims.

The would-be victim told the police that the woman in question drove a pale Renault. That information led the authorities to Mahin, who had a yellow car matching that description and had paid a fine for her role in a vehicle crash in the not-so-distant past. Serial killers are often caught in surprisingly prosaic ways, and Mahin's reign of terror ended thanks to a simple traffic violation.

The news reports do not explain what happened when Mahin was taken in for questioning. Presumably, her would-be victim identified her, but it is not known how long Mahin was interrogated for, or what caused her to make a confession, or how long it took for her to admit her own guilt.

When Mahin confessed, she explained that she had developed a set routine for killing her victims. She would find a woman in her mature years, often a senior citizen. She would meet them coming home from shrines and offer them a ride home in her car. Often, she would make comments about how these women reminded her of her own mother. Some news reports accused Mahin of playing "mind games" with her passengers, though no examples of what constituted a "mind game" were provided. At some point in the ride, the victim was offered some fruit juice that had been laced with a powerful drug. Once the victim fell into unconsciousness, Mahin would kill her, take the victim's jewelry and everything else of value, and then leave the corpse in a secluded area. If the potential fifth victim had not outwitted Mahin, it is possible that many more women could have died.

There is nothing readily available to prove what Mahin looked like. The image of a veiled woman attached to some news stories may be Mahin, but the image shows only a black-garbed woman using her cuffed hands to pull her hijab over her face. None of the woman's features are discernable. Only a small patch of forehead and a tuft of dark hair are visible. The photograph may even possibly be a stock photo. The *Irish Times* did provide a very brief description of Mahin as a woman with a strong frame, toughened by her experience with track and field. This *Irish Times* report also stated that Mahin had two children, although no other details about them were provided, such as their names or their father. The only other fact known for sure about Mahin was her age. At the time of her arrest, Mahin was thirty-two years old.

The authorities had some theories as to what caused Mahin to become a killer. In a *Guardian* report, Ali Akbar Hedayati, the police chief of Qazvin, stated that Mahin was mentally ill, a condition that was precipitated by the fact that her mother failed to provide her with the necessary love and emotional support to function in a healthy manner. Hedayati declared that, "It is likely that the murderer took revenge on women who resembled her mother and were of the same age because of her intense hatred of her own mother." The concept of a serial killer becoming homicidal due to a damaged maternal relationship is hardly a new one, as anybody familiar with the novel or movie *Psycho* will know.

Mahin's motives likely went beyond mental illness connected to her estrangement from her mother. Money was another reason for the crimes. Some news reports insist that financial considerations were the primary reason for the murders, rather than pathological loathing for her parent. In her confessions, Mahin revealed that she was over £16,000 (approximately $24,000 at the contemporaneous rate of exchange) in debt, and stealing her victims' valuables was her only way to regain her financial stability. While her monetary troubles explain the need for theft, it does not explain why she found homicide to be necessary. After all, many burglars steal large sums of money and property without having to resort to lethal violence. Mahin's debt only explains why she became a thief. It does not adequately explain why she chose to become a killer.

After her arrest, Mahin reportedly confessed to two additional murders: those of her aunt and her former landlord. The latter was her only known male victim, and these crimes took place before she targeted female strangers. The means by which she killed her first two victims are unknown, and it is similarly not known how Mahin escaped suspicion and arrest for the deaths of two people with a direct connection to her.

Few details of Mahin's trial are known. What is clear is that Mahin was convicted, and in 2011, Mahin met the same fate as many of the murderers in Christie's novels before the abolition of capital punishment in Britain—she was executed by hanging.

Additionally, two men were arrested for selling Mahin the sedatives she used to knock out her victims. Their fates are not recounted in the news coverage connected to Mahin.

With Mahin's execution, the news coverage of her crimes ended. No further details of her life, the deaths she caused, her family members, or anything about her victims was released to the western news media.

All western audiences trying to follow the case received were a few very brief quotes from press releases. The prosecutor Mohammad Baqer Olfat announced to the media that "Mahin in her confessions said that she has been taking patterns from Agatha Christie books and has been trying not to leave any trace of herself." As the footprint mentioned earlier indicates, Mahin was not as scrupulous in eliminating incriminating forensic evidence as she ought to have been. Mahin did succeed in leaving no clear traces of which Agatha Christie's books gave her inspiration.

Due to the limited details about Mahin's crimes, there are a great many unanswered questions about the specifics of the murders. It is unclear, for example, exactly which Agatha Christie books Mahin read and which lessons she learned from them. *Evil Under the Sun* and *The Body in the Library*, for example, feature deaths by strangulation and unusually creative alibis. There is, however, nothing in the news reports to indicate which Christie stories were twisted to suit Mahin's violent ends. Neither is it known for sure if she was actually trying to duplicate crimes from Christie's books or if she simply derived inspiration from a handful of minor plot points.

It is certainly possible that one of Christie's books may have given Mahin the idea to drug her victims before killing them. Novels like *And Then There were None*, *The Body in the Library*, and *After the Funeral* are just a few of Christie's novels that feature murders where the victim has been given a dose of some powerful soporific before being slain. Of course, Mahin could easily have gotten that idea from any number of other sources besides Christie books.

Indeed, given the little that is known outside of Iran regarding Mahin's murder spree, one cannot be sure if the serial killer was even inspired by actual Agatha Christie novels. Recently, a Middle Eastern publisher released a novel with Christie's name prominently displayed on it, and the text was translated into Arabic. The title of this book was *The Fingerprints*. There is no official Christie novel title of that name or anything close to that, though publishers around the world, especially in the United States, have made a habit of changing Christie's titles to whatever they like whenever it suits their whims. *The Fingerprints*, however, was actually the novel *The Murder of the Clergyman's Mistress* by Anthony Abbot (a pseudonym for the author Fulton Oursler, best known for his religious writings). Apparently, the publisher simply took a translation of an obscure American detective story, and slapped Christie's name on it in order to boost sales. It is highly probable that neither the estates of Christie nor Abbot ever saw a penny of the profits of this misidentified edition.

"Counterfeit novels" are a booming business in many parts of the world. In China, the many instances of fanfiction being passed off as actual Harry Potter novels have become a subgenre all of their own. Indeed, in one instance, J.R.R. Tolkien's *The Hobbit* was passed off as a new Harry Potter story in China, with Harry replacing Bilbo Baggins and Dumbledore taking Gandalf's role. There's no way of knowing if something comparable happened in Iran, with Mahin reading some other author's work in translation, sold under the Christie name. It is possible that Mahin got ideas from ersatz Christies, but that is pure speculation.

Whatever the true source of inspiration for Mahin's crimes was, it's worth noting that Christie's works have also saved the lives of real-life people. The most famous examples come from Christie's novel *The Pale Horse*, where the side effects of thallium poisoning were described in graphic detail. This information caused Christie fans to recognize the symptoms in real-life patients, such as a baby who accidentally consumed thallium, and a man being poisoned by his wife.

The most famous instance of Christie's *The Pale Horse* preventing deaths by thallium is the case of Graham Frederick Young, a serial killer known as "The Bovington Bug" and "The Teacup Killer," who murdered at least three individuals with thallium. When Christie first heard about Young's crimes, her first response was reportedly one of worry– she feared that her books had given a troubled man the information he needed to take innocent lives. Further investigation proved that Christie had no reason to reproach herself. Young was not inspired by Christie's books– he was sickening people with poison long before *The Pale Horse* was published, but his case illustrates how

ESSAY: THE AGATHA CHRISTIE SERIAL KILLER

Christie's books can be a useful tool in catching serial killers.

It should be noted that there are not very many murderers who fit the current definition of serial killers in Christie's novels. Her most famous serial killer is found in *The ABC Murders*. The villain of that story travels the country killing people in alphabetical order, in locations that match their initials. *By the Pricking of My Thumbs* does feature a serial killer who poisons children and the occasional adult. These fictional multiple murderers do match the contemporary definition of a serial killer as someone who commits at minimum three murders over a period of time longer than a month, with the slayings spaced out over an extended time frame. In other Christie novels, like *And Then There were None*, *A Murder is Announced*, and *The Mirror Crack'd* the murders take place over a fairly short period of time. In the case of *And Then There were None*, the killer orchestrates ten deaths and then commits suicide over the course of a single weekend. In *Death Comes as the End*, the killer of over half a dozen people is closer to a family annihilator than the standard definition of a serial killer. Most of Christie's murderers only kill one or two people at most, sometimes more if accidents require them to silence a witness.

Looking critically at the news reports, it is worth questioning whether or not the moniker of "The Agatha Christie Serial Killer" is an accurate title. Many law enforcement officers balk at giving multiple murderers catchy nicknames, claiming that the practice glamorizes these atrocious crimes. To cite just one example, in 2009, soon after Mahin's capture, the city of Milwaukee, Wisconsin was hit by the revelation that a serial killer had been operating in its midst for over two decades. DNA evidence identified Walter E. Ellis as having sexually assaulted and throttled seven African-American women during this time. There were some questions in the media about how Ellis had been allowed to keep taking lives for so long, but the main controversy lay in how some of Milwaukee's most prominent news outlets bestowed the moniker of "The North Side Strangler" upon him.

Milwaukee commentator Eugene Kane declared, "Frankly, I don't think he deserves a catchy nickname... Giving him a nickname just adds a tabloid element to media coverage and adds to the grief of families caught up in the latest revelations about the loss of their loved ones. These are human beings, after all. It's not a made-for-TV miniseries. (FYI: Don't blame the anchors or reporters who say this stuff: The media's decision to name serial killers usually is made far above their heads.)"

Based on the news coverage, it's possible that the Agatha Christie connection was played up as a "hook" to drum up attention for the story. Given the lack of direct links between Christie's plots and Mahin's crimes, it is highly likely that the connection was a more tenuous one. We know that this was not a case of Mahin deliberately replicating the most colorful murders from Christie's oeuvre, such as stabbing a man twelve times on a train, killing a woman with a blowgun dart dipped in snake venom, or rigging a chessboard to electrocute a player, and then leaving behind copies of *Murder on the Orient Express*, *Death in the Clouds*, and *The Big Four* at the scenes of these respective crimes, much like Christie's fictional serial killer left behind ABC railway guides near his victims in *The ABC Murders*.

Indeed, given what we know about Mahin's murders— four nearly-identical drugging-and-smothering slayings of middle-aged to elderly women (aside from one bludgeoning when the soporific drug didn't work as planned), it does not appear that Mahin borrowed too many actual plot points from Christie's work. In *Nemesis* a victim is strangled, disfigured, and left in an isolated place. Also, in *Dead Man's Folly*, the mystery writer Ariadne Oliver (often considered to be Christie's self-parody) has her plotline for a "murder hunt" game hijacked by a real killer who strangles a teenaged girl. There is no Christie novel where various elderly women are drugged, smothered or strangled, robbed, and abandoned in out-of-the-way areas. All in all, Mahin's crimes do not match Christie's books (at least Mahin's targeting of women coming home from religious services– nothing has been revealed of how Mahin's aunt and ex-landlord met their deaths), and it is possible that Mahin only learned a few simple lessons on how to avoid detection from Christie's books, and that the serial killer's connection to the Queen of Crime was overblown by the media in order to create a more eye-catching story.

Would Mahin's case have made international headlines if she had been known simply as "The Senior Citizen Smotherer" or "The Monster of Qazvin?" It is probable that Mahin's infamy was in part due to being linked to a beloved, world-renowned crime writer, even though the news reports provided no clear evidence of just how Christie's mysteries were incorporated into Mahin's murderous plans. The news coverage was notable for its cursory presentation of specific details– none of the six victims were ever named in the English-language news coverage of the time.

If Mahin's murders were inspired by fiction, it is certainly possible that in the future Mahin's murders might inspire fiction as well. Real-life serial killers have long been creative fodder for crime novelists and screenwriters. Ed Gein, the grisly murderer from Plainfield, Wisconsin, has famously inspired not just the character of Norman Bates from *Psycho*, but also the character of Jame Gumb from *The Silence of the Lambs*, Leatherface from *The Texas Chain Saw Massacre* and Bloody Face from *American Horror Story: Asylum*, as well as several other lesser-known cases. An incident where the Milwaukee-based cannibal Jeffrey Dahmer escaped arrest by police was fictionalized into the play *A Steady Rain*, starring Hugh Jackman and Daniel Craig on Broadway. The crimes of Jack the Ripper have spawned their own genre of crime entertainment inspired by the Whitechapel murders. Indeed, the *Law & Order* franchise has made episodes "ripped from the headlines" of crime news its personal hallmark.

There are countless other examples of writers adapting actual crimes as a source of inspiration, and it is certainly possible that some enterprising mystery writer may turn to Mahin for ideas. Perhaps in the years to come, the sparse facts of the case we know will be fictionalized and spun into a movie or television production.

Given the current political situation, it is unlikely that Western true crime aficionados will learn all of the true details of Mahin's crimes, unless an Iranian writer is inclined and able to write a thorough account of her rampage, and that project would subsequently get translated into English and made available to Western publishers. Until then, people outside of Iran are unlikely to know the true connection between a serial killer and the world's bestselling mystery writer.

THE JOYRIDE

LEAH R CUTTER

Miki loved the smell of expensive new cars. The plastic scent that still blew in from the vents. How the smell of the cream-colored leather seats promised buttery smoothness and instant warmth. Burled oak decorated the dash, still shiny from the factory, adding to the heady perfume, a hint of woods underneath it all.

She drove her "borrowed" ride down the tree-lined streets of the suburbs of Chicago, past expansive lawns and mansions. Spring was in its final phases, the air still crisp and the grass brilliant green. She couldn't see the lake past the houses—the rich fucks were too greedy to allow passerbys a view. She knew it was there, though. Her own rich fuck had quite a spread just a few blocks away, and threw private parties during the summer just to show it off.

A cop car suddenly lit up its cherries behind her.

Startled, Miki tightened her fingers on the steering wheel. Edward hadn't reported the car as stolen, had he? No, he wasn't home yet. Didn't know it was missing.

She glanced down at the speedometer. She was doing the speed limit. What did the pig want?

She quickly eased the car to the side.

The cops sped past her, intent on ruining someone else's day.

Miki sat where she was next to the curb for a moment, breathing deeply, trying to calm her racing heart.

Her life was no longer filled with worry about the cops, either to arrest her for solicitation or to force her out of whatever squat she currently occupied.

No, she'd managed to hitch a ride uptown. Edward was a good sugar daddy, though he wasn't that sweet. And she knew how to play him, to turn sourness into playfulness, or when to just hold him and listen.

Honest to fuck, that was what he seemed to appreciate most of all sometimes.

Though the constant access to "eager" pussy didn't hurt.

She kept herself in shape for him, too. Did all the Pilates and squats, a constant regime of creams to keep her white skin flawless and young. Wore skin-tight leggings and stretchy tops to show off her enhancements, like today's outfit of a dove-gray T-shirt embellished with white flowers, black skinny jeans, and killer black heels.

Miki drummed her fingers against the heated steering wheel for a moment, thinking.

She really had come a long way in her twenty-seven years.

Slowly, she pulled back into the street, taking a left, then another, aiming the car in the opposite direction.

Originally, she hadn't had any plan for this joyride. Technically, she hadn't stolen the car. Just borrowed it for the afternoon, let the wind from the open sunroof tease her dyed blonde hair, nowhere to go, nothing to do, just ride.

Sure, Edward might fuss at her when she came back. She wasn't supposed to take his car without permission. It wasn't like she was on the insurance or anything.

But she'd call him Teddy, let him playfully growl at her. She might even offer to put on the French maid's outfit for the evening—just a fancy collar and a corset—then walk around with a feather duster, leaning over again and again to dust a spec of something from the floor, giving him a good eyeful.

Now, though, Miki was filled with a strange longing: to see the old neighborhood. Where she'd come from.

She didn't need to be motivated by it. She already knew she never, *ever*, wanted to live like that again. She didn't have many good memories of the place.

Yet, she found herself making turn after turn, getting onto the busy highway then off again, heading south, always south.

Gonna take a joyride in the old town.

Miki had watched the news. Seen the footage of the riots from when the cops had been caught being killers.

Knew nothing would change. Hadn't been disappointed by that.

Still, she found a strange gratification driving down these streets and realizing that it didn't look like a warzone anymore. Not exactly.

Sure, there were homeless encampments—the warmer weather drove those bugs outside. The few shops that were still open along the street hid behind well-fortified iron grates. Colorful graffiti bloomed like the flowers in the burbs; some gang markings, mostly tags. A few buildings on one block had been burned from the inside out and never demolished. Insurance money probably wouldn't cover it.

So it wasn't that nice of a place. The onslaught of gentrification only nibbled at the edges. It wasn't a neighborhood, either, the way people shied away from each other as they passed on the sidewalk.

However, it hadn't turned into hell. Not like just a few blocks away where there were only the homeless and despair.

Miki turned down a quiet street, hoping to catch a glimpse of the one apartment building she'd stayed in that had been halfway decent. She had to circle a few times, trying to remember which one had been it.

She knew if she got out and walk the street, her feet would remember. Or maybe her nose would direct her.

But she didn't want to leave the safe armor of her car.

Edward's car.

Whatever.

As she approached one of the tagged and dinged stop signs again, a boy darted out from nowhere, directly in front of her car.

Miki felt more than heard the thump of her bumper hitting him.

He was nowhere in sight.

Shit. Had she run over him?

She threw the car into park and quickly let herself out, heading toward the front of the car.

Some well-honed instinct made her look over her shoulder before she got there.

Just in time to see a well-muscled black guy in a khaki military jacket slide into the driver's seat.

"Oh no you don't," Miki said. She didn't bother trying to open the driver's door. Though she worked out and kept her muscles toned, she knew instinctively that she couldn't compete with this asshole.

Instead, she threw herself into the backseat as he floored it, the motion slamming the door behind her.

"Well, lookie here," the driver said, grinning at her in the rearview mirror. "See who's decided to join us."

It was only then that Miki noticed that he had a companion, the little black kid, seated in the passenger seat. The child was maybe ten years old, wearing a ripped black jacket. He held a gun with two hands, pointed right at her chest. The weapon looked ridiculously large in his tiny black hands, but he held it steady.

"Think we might have just picked up a golden ticket!" the asshole driver continued. "How much do you think her owner will pay to get her back?"

THE JOYRIDE

"What, you think you're kidnapping me?" Miki said. She gave a snort of derision. "I ain't worth nothing. No one's gonna pay."

She pressed her lips together, unwilling to let anymore words slip out. She'd worked so hard on flattening out her accent until she sounded like all those people in the rich enclaves.

Not like a gutter-whore from the south side.

"Whatcha mean? Sweet ride like this? Like you? Someone's gonna wanna pay," the asshole continued.

"No. He won't," Miki said. "Don't you know nothin' about rich people? They ain't like us." She paused, considering her words, and changing her accent again. "It isn't about the car. It's about getting the best and newest. Hell, he'd probably thank you for taking it away just as the new models are coming out. This car, this thing, means nothing to him. He could have ten more just like it delivered in the morning."

Miki paused again. "And a hundred more like me by noon."

She'd always known she was replaceable. As soon as her beauty ran out, she'd be out of luck. Aged out, as it were.

Edward never really kept track of all the cash

he gave her, though, and she could scrimp and save in ways he never considered.

He wouldn't be her last ride. He was generous, but not that much.

No, he'd trade her in for a younger model eventually. Then she'd have to hitch herself to another guy and ride him for all he was worth. Maybe then she'd have enough.

"Okay, going back to the original plan, then," the guy said, making an abrupt right turn.

Miki thought for a moment. "Gonna drop this piece into Jace's lap, then?"

The guy caught her eye in the rearview mirror. "What you talking about?" he asked suspiciously.

"Jace Morre. Runs a chop shop two blocks away," Miki said. "I used to live here." She added, "Drop me off just outside the garage. I need to be able to tell the owner that I don't have any idea what happened to the car."

The black guy nodded and did just that, stopping at the corner to let her off, then driving the car into the open garage door of the next building.

Miki took a deep breath and considered her next options. She had to get back, had to tell Edward...something.

Just wearing the little French maid's outfit probably wasn't going to cut it.

It surprised her when the black guy came sauntering out of the garage and walked over to where she was standing.

"Dewar," he said with a nod.

"Like the scotch?" Miki asked, her tone derisive.

But Dewar just shrugged. "Good as any."

"I'm Miki," she said, because that name was as good as any as well.

Neither of the names just exchanged had originally appeared on either of their birth certificates, she was certain.

"You good?" Dewar asked. He seemed more curious than concerned.

Or maybe he was just checking to make sure that she wasn't about to call the cops on the shop.

Miki found herself talking again, even though she really didn't mean to. "I spent a lot of years here, on these streets," she said. She leaned her back against the rough brick of the building beside her, her voice dropping. "Don't want to be back here."

And maybe that was why she'd had to take her joyride that afternoon.

To discover what she was not.

Dewar nodded, resting his bulk beside hers. "But you got out."

"I did," Miki said. "Don't you want to?"

Dewar shrugged. "It's good enough for now."

Miki nodded. He didn't need to hear anything from her about the dangers of his current occupation. No matter how good he might be boosting cars, he was always going to be at the mercy of the weakest link in his supply chain.

He'd do time, eventually. She could see that acceptance in his stance.

Maybe then he'd figure out what he wasn't.

Now, though, Miki had to get back to that grand life of hers, the bubble that protected her from getting carjacked or fucked over.

At least by someone other than Edward.

This was gonna suck.

But she had to sell the story she'd started spinning in her head.

She glanced at Dewar, pushed herself up, and took a step to bring her closer to the corner of the building. She slid her right palm over the gritty brick to the very edge of the building, with just her nails resting on the surface. Then she pushed her hand forward, *hard*.

Two nails broke all the way off, the pain sending a shiver down her arm. The third just cracked in half.

"Fuck!" Miki said. She shook her hand, but

didn't allow herself to stop. She immediately jammed her right elbow into the brick, then slid her arm across it, giving her forearm a good abrasion.

"Damn, girl," Dewar said with something like admiration in his voice.

"Gotta sell it," Miki said. "I was carjacked, but I fought. I fought for his piece of shit car." She faced Dewar squarely. "You need to hit me. Twice. Left side of the face. Once to make my lip bleed, and a second time to give me a shiner."

"Ya sure about that?" Dewar asked.

"I am," Miki said, nodding.

Before she could back down, Dewar jabbed out. She tried not to flinch, but still did. The blow landed solidly on the corner of her mouth.

The second hit came before she'd had a chance to recover. She let it carry her to the ground, onto her right side, making sure to get dirt on her jeans. And, oh look! A tear there too, which she tore at, making it wider.

"You okay?" Dewar said, coming to stand over her.

She nodded, holding up her left hand to him, so he could help her up. Her right hand was still smarting too much.

"You did good. Thanks," she told him, with a

crooked smile. That left side of her face was already starting to hurt and swell up.

"Where you going?" Dewar asked as she turned and started walking away.

Miki paused. "Not going to call an Uber until I'm four blocks away, at a corner where they'll actually pick me up. Wouldn't do for me to call for a ride just outside of a known chop shop."

Edward wasn't the brightest, but he wasn't dumb either. He couldn't see her location on her phone—she kept it turned off—but he might think to look up where she'd gotten into her Uber.

Miki hurried down the blocks, never making eye-contact, heading back toward an area where people would possibly smile when they walked down the street.

She spied a well-known bakery, still open after all these years, and made her call for the Uber after she stepped inside the shop.

When she stepped back outside, she had a box of world-famous sesame seed donuts in one hand and her ride was waiting.

The drive back up to the safe, rich enclaves left Miki in thought.

Just running away from everything back there

in her old neighborhood had been good enough for years.

That strange compulsion to go back to see her old haunts hadn't been just to reminisce about the shitty times she'd had there.

No, it was to remind her that she could do more now that she had escaped. Not just survive, but thrive.

She broke off the right heel of her shoe, then instructed the driver to let her off at the curb instead of taking the long drive up to the house, past the manicured lawn.

She kept the heel of her broken shoe in one hand, the box of donuts in her other, as she limped up the asphalt.

Had to sell it.

Someday, though, she was going to get off this ride.

And maybe instead, go looking for her joy.

COOL RIDE

DIANA DEVERELL

Ted Tarrant stood motionless on the concrete path. The toes of his black running shoes were five inches beyond the reach of the streetlight on Cherry Way. Surveying his surroundings, Ted felt a zing of elation. He'd picked the perfect spot to launch tonight's joyride.

The path crossed an undeveloped scrap of land between the east end of Cherry Way and the adjacent north-south artery called Good Farm Road. The path was designed for use by kids biking or walking to a nearby elementary school. A bollard at each end of the path blocked cars from entering.

Ted let his gaze pass over the six single-family houses lining the Cherry Way cul-de-sac. At one-thirty in the morning on this second Tuesday in May, he saw no sign that any of the homeowners living in the cul-de-sac were awake. The car they planned to steal was parked in the driveway of the middle house on the north side of the cul-de-sac. Which meant their joyride would begin with a straight shot west on Cherry Way, with no immediate risk of pursuit from behind.

Ted wore a black long-sleeved T-shirt paired with black jeans. He'd pulled a black knit cap over his shaggy silver hair. Not likely that the pale skin on his hands and clean-shaven face would catch the eye of anyone looking his way.

A cricket chirped and new leaves on the two decrepit filbert trees still alive in the dirt beside the path rustled softly. Ted patted his stomach, satisfyingly full of the double cheeseburger and fries he grabbed on the way to rendezvous with Jeff Randall. Jack-in-the-Box kept its drive-thru open till 3:00 AM and the lone person on duty was happy to serve Ted as a walk-thru customer. The delicious flavors of hot beef, cheese, and grease lingered on his tongue and his fingers smelled like salty potatoes.

Ted felt a hand on his elbow. A stocky five-foot-ten, he completely blocked the shorter, thinner black-clad man who stood behind him. Ted had connected with Jeff Randall five minutes ago at the Good Farm Road end of the path. He and Jeff both wore black, same as when they were fourteen years old and sneaking out their bedroom windows to joyride under cover of darkness.

"The Mustang in the driveway?" Jeff rasped in his smoke-damaged voice.

"Take a look." Ted shuffled to his left, making room for Jeff beside him. "Snugged up to the garage door," he added as he admired the sleek black exterior of the 1966 Mustang. "Very kind of

Hazel North to make this classic beauty available to us."

"Very stupid, you mean." Jeff barked a disparaging laugh. "You said you blocked the receiver on her garage door opener this afternoon while she was gone in her car. When she got home and the door didn't open, why didn't she go into the garage and push the button manually?"

"Not Hazel's style," Ted replied. "I tested my little trick on her last Friday. When the door didn't move, she hopped out of her car, locked it up, and went through her front door into the house. Guess she doesn't like dragging her eighty-five-year-old body in and out of the car. I made sure she found that her garage door opener was back in working order the next morning. She probably thinks this is another temporary glitch."

Jeff patted the plastic handle of the Craftsman screwdriver tucked into the waistband of his jeans. "You said we don't need a tool but I brought this in case you were wrong. Useless for hotwiring new cars, but should do the trick on one this old."

Ted shrugged. "Last week when I checked, Hazel's spare key was in a magnetic holder behind the front license plate. I imagine it still is. But good you brought a reliable backup."

As kids, they'd jammed a screwdriver into an

ignition to turn it on. Worked as well as a key most of the time. Probably wrecked some ignitions, but that didn't affect them. Joyriding was one smooth, unbroken trip, they didn't have to start a car more than once. Still, it was better if they left behind no evidence that someone had borrowed the car.

Ted rubbed his hands together in anticipation. "Damn, I can't wait to drive this baby."

"So you said," Jeff replied. "I don't get why it's a big deal for you. You must've driven a Mustang before."

Ted shrugged. "The Mustang isn't the point. What I miss is the thrill of doing what's forbidden without getting caught. When we were fourteen, we couldn't legally drive, or drink, or smoke. Had to break the law to have any fun. Hell, breaking the law was half of the fun itself. Since I lost my license and I gave up alcohol and tobacco, I'm back in the same boat. And willing to try a few forbidden things to spice things up."

Jeff snorted. "Getting old must be really boring for you. I'm seventy-eight, same as you, but I have a vice or two left to spice up my life." He pulled a quarter out of his jeans pocket. "I'll flip, you call. Like the old days."

Jeff flipped.

Ted said, "Heads."

"Tails," Jeff crowed. "I drive first."

Exactly like the old days. Ted managed not to grin.

In the past, nine times out of ten, Jeff won the coin toss. Or claimed he did. Once again, the toss put Jeff behind the wheel, right where Ted wanted him tonight. He was glad he could count on Jeff's predictability. And criminal disposition.

When they were kids, Ted's dad had warned him that Jeff was bad company. True then, true now.

Their standard operating procedure was that only one of them got in the car to start the engine. The other jogged to a nearby intersection and stood lookout, signaling the driver to abort the mission if anyone showed up to witness their crime. Their getaway plan was to run like hell in opposite directions, making it impossible for a single onlooker to catch them both. The one time that happened, they both got away. If they got interrupted tonight, one of them could escape via the bike path and no car could follow.

Ted headed toward the intersection where Cherry Way crossed Filbert Lane. Hurrying silently along the sidewalk past darkened houses, he inhaled the sweet spring breeze caressing his face. He'd loved growing up in this mid-sized Oregon town. His mom and dad weren't pleased by what he got up to with Jeff. Still, he managed to graduate from high school. And he served only one year in the state prison for first offenders aged eighteen to twenty. Course, that was all on Jeff.

Ted reached the corner of Cherry and Filbert and stepped behind a large rhododendron, his dark clothing blending in with the shiny green leaves. He had a plan for tonight but he wasn't in control of all the pieces. He had to be ready to salvage the operation if things fell apart.

Ted heard the soft purr of the Mustang engine starting up. Checked back the way he'd come and saw the white backup lights glow on the Mustang's rear.

Glancing south on Filbert, he spotted a police cruiser facing him. All lights off, engine idling softly. His shoulders dropped in relief. Little brother Pete had come through for him. A retired cop, Pete had tipped off the local PD to the probability that around 1:30 AM, they'd get a 911 call from Hazel North reporting a thief breaking into her car.

Backing away from the cruiser and moving behind the rhodie, Ted's gaze went to the Mustang. Jeff had reversed onto Cherry and the car's front end was pointed toward the intersection. The Mustang shot forward as if Jeff had floored the accelerator.

The cruiser moved quickly, too. The powerful engine growled, blue light flashed, and the siren whooped. The cruiser reached the center of the intersection in seconds.

Tires squealed as Jeff hit the brakes. He must've yanked the wheel to the left because the Mustang bounced over that curb and plowed across an empty driveway onto a lush lawn, stopping inches from a fifteen-foot-tall pine tree.

Ted watched as Jeff threw open the driver's door, leapt out of the car, and dashed across the lawn into the street. Jeff headed away from the cruiser, toward the path.

A uniformed police officer materialized under the streetlight at the near-end of the path. Behind him, blue lights flashed on a second cruiser parked on Good Farm Road.

Jeff stopped and turned around, checking for an escape route past the cruiser in the intersection. Another cop stood beside the hood, the weapon in his hand pointed down.

Boxed in by two cops, Jeff turned his head from side to side, searching for a way around them. One of the cops shouted, ordering Jeff down on his knees with his hands in the air.

Ted realized that the cops were connected wirelessly and talking to each other. Most likely, the cop who waited on the path had surveilled Jeff. Hiding beyond the reach of the streetlight, that cop saw Jeff take the car key from the magnetic key holder, unlock the doors, enter the Mustang, and start the engine. That cop had told the cruiser driver when to make his blocking maneuver.

Jeff had to realize he couldn't get away through the side and back yards of the adjacent houses. A pair of cops in their twenties would easily overtake a seventy-eight-year-old man trying to clamber over backyard fences.

As Ted expected, Jeff sank to his knees and raised both hands in the air. While the cops were busy frisking and cuffing him, Ted silently turned the corner and headed north on Filbert Lane. At the next cul-de-sac, he turned right and slipped between a pair of houses on his right until he reached the fence at the back of Hazel's house.

Ted carefully opened a well-oiled and squeak-free gate and stepped into Hazel's back yard. Closing the gate behind him, he moved soundlessly onto a covered deck furnished with a cushioned recliner, a small glass-topped table, and a pair of red-and-black folding chairs. A tall, flowering lilac perfumed the air.

Ted checked his watch. 1:45 AM. The cops would keep Hazel busy for at least another hour. He stretched out on the recliner, setting off squishy farts from the cushions. Closed his eyes and fell asleep.

He woke to a soft female voice crooning, "Time to get up, Ted."

Opening his eyes, he saw that sunshine lit the patch of lawn beyond his feet. The voice belonged to Hazel Jones, a petite woman with salt-and-pepper curls topping her head. She wore a lightweight jacket of soft black leather over a lavender blouse and khaki slacks. Ted knew that Hazel was eight years older than he was, but to him, she didn't look a day over sixty.

"Good morning, Ted," Hazel said. "I have some questions I hope you're ready to answer."

Ted moved his feet to the ground and sat up. "First, I have a question for you. Did that asshole damage your Mustang?"

Hazel's negative head shake set her curls bobbing. "Not a scratch. Though he nearly hit that tree. Why do you think he gunned it like that?"

Ted laughed. "To answer your questions

about last night, we have to go back to the question that brought us to this point. Remember, you asked me if my old buddy Jeff Randall was casing your house for a burglary?"

Hazel sniffed. "Not an unreasonable concern when a notorious juvenile delinquent follows me home from the grocery store and spends ten minutes eyeing my place from his parked car."

Ted shook his head. "Been a long time since you last saw Jeff. I'm amazed you recognized him."

"I'm good with faces," Hazel replied. "Remember, I recognized you the minute you caught up with me when I was out walking. That look in your eyes gave you away."

Ted chuckled. "The one you claim signals *I am up to no good and having the time of my life.*"

"Signaled," Hazel corrected. "That's how I read it when you were young. This morning, I see only a charming twinkle in your grown-up law-abiding eyes."

"I'm flattered," Ted said. "And pleased you find me law-abiding."

"Wouldn't have left my car out on the driveway last night if I didn't," Hazel retorted. "I confess that I did not identify Jeff as quickly. Took a couple of minutes to remember his name. You were sure I was mistaken. Last you heard, he moved to Portland."

"And I moved to Phoenix," Ted said. "He and I lost touch. When I reached retirement age, I was single again and my two kids were off seeing the world. I moved back here to be near my little brother Pete."

"Is he still a cop?" Hazel asked.

"Retired, but he keeps up with things," Ted replied. "Pete confirmed Jeff is back in town. I described Jeff's interest in your house. Pete said that most likely Jeff kept returning to your place because he was figuring out how to steal your Mustang."

"Right," Hazel said. "You told me Pete's cop pals think Jeff's responsible for half a dozen car thefts in the area but they lack any evidence incriminating him."

Her eyes widened. "Last night, I did what you told me to do. Left the Mustang in the driveway, got comfy in the dark living room, and kept an eye on the driveway. When a man dressed in black showed up, I called 911."

"You were perfect," Ted said.

"You mean the trap you set was perfect," Hazel retorted. "But how did you get Jeff to take the bait?"

"I tracked him down. Told him I'd heard he'd returned. Said that I'd spotted a 1966 Mustang I planned to take for a joyride. Invited him to come with me. Mentioned your address as the car's location."

Hazel rolled her eyes. "Highly improbable that a man your age would want to go joyriding. I'm surprised Jeff bought your nonsense."

"I could tell Jeff thought it was a dumb idea," Ted said. "But since I claimed I could guarantee the Mustang would be in the driveway, he acted like he was up for a joyride, too. He wanted your car and he saw no risk in involving me. Dumb Ted could never pull a fast one on smart Jeff. Probably thought he'd outfoxed me when he rigged the coin toss to make him driver and send me down the street as lookout."

"The cop who took my statement didn't say one word about you," Hazel said.

Ted held out his arms to display his all-black attire. "I did my best to become invisible."

"You succeeded," Hazel shook her head. "And you answered my question as to why Jeff gunned the engine. He never intended to take you for a ride. That was why he hit the gas so hard. He was going to blow right past you."

"You're right," Ted agreed. "The big money in

car theft these days is selling off the catalytic converter and other parts. Stripping the car immediately makes it difficult to nail the thief. Jeff was hell-bent on driving your car straight to his mechanic pals at the chop shop before any cops spotted him."

Hazel beamed at him. "I appreciate you going to all that trouble to protect me and my car."

Ted shook his head. "Wasn't entirely a selfless act. Jeff owed me for something he did in the past. Last night I collected."

Hazel made a dismissive wave. "Let me thank you for what you did for me by treating you to the breakfast special at Carl's Jr."

"I accept." Ted chuckled. "I can't say no to anything on Carl's menu."

"I knew that," Hazel said. "You told me fast food is one of your three great loves."

Ted stood, pulled off his stocking cap and tucked it into the back pocket of his jeans. "Did the cops impound the Mustang?"

"They did," Hazel replied. "But I have another car I inherited from my husband. Of course, his car had to be cooler than mine."

"I'm sure no car is cooler than your Mustang," Ted said.

"Follow me and decide for yourself." Hazel

opened the back door to her house. She led him through a galley kitchen and past a round oak pedestal table with matching cushioned chairs and down a short hallway to the door to the garage. She pulled it open and flipped a light switch.

The space on the left side was empty. On the right sat a shiny silver four-door sedan. The medallion on the grill featured a jungle cat.

"A Jaguar." Ted narrowed his eyes. "Is that the Super V8 model?"

"It is," Hazel said. A 2005 XJ 8, to be precise."

"Three hundred ninety horsepower. Zero to sixty in a touch over five seconds." Tad's sigh was flavored with reverence. "No question, this Jag is cooler than your Mustang. I am one lucky man. Fast cars are another of my great loves."

Hazel laughed. "If you're like most men, fast women are the remaining great love on your list."

Not eager to grouped in the *most men* category, Ted instantly revised his mental list. "At my age?" he snorted. "No, fast friends are my third great love. You know who I mean. Fun people like you."

He pushed a button on the wall and the garage door slowly rose. "Come on," he said to Hazel. "Let's take a ride in your Jag."

THE VANISHING CONVERTIBLE

CATE MARTIN

January 11, 1938, St. Paul, Minnesota

A lot of private investigator work had to, by its very nature, take place after dark. So Dottie Lundegaard liked to open up the office in the morning on her own and let her brother sleep in another hour or two without worrying about missing any potential, much-needed clients.

It was handy that the one-room apartment that they shared was just a flight of steep, uneven stairs up from his office. She could throw on her clothes in the dark, then creep down those steps in her stockinged-feet to start the coffee before using the little mirror behind the coat rack to arrange her brown hair neatly.

Then she had to go out to fetch the paper. That was the only hardship in any of it. Because as many times as she had complained to the people at the paper, every time with them whole-heartedly agreeing that what she and her brother paid for delivery meant delivery through the mail slot in their office door, the paperboy always just chucked it into the alley from the main street beyond. It seldom cleared the dumpster that stood outside the restaurant's kitchen door, let alone beyond the restaurant to their office stoop.

In the summer, this was irritating because of the smells that emanated from that dumpster. For the life of her, Dottie didn't understand how a restaurant who had nothing with cabbage in it on their menu could throw so much of it away. And always in such a rotted state.

But things weren't much better now, in the middle of January. Granted, the deep chill of the last week had definitely precluded any food smells. The air had been so frigid it would have frozen the inside of her nose if she hadn't kept her wool scarf up over it. Which was good for avoiding odor, but bad for just about anything else.

Just a short trip to the end of the alley and back would leave her huddled, still in her coat, as close as she could get to the radiator, a mug of that hot if not particularly good coffee clutched in her numb hands.

The best she could do was try to be quick. So after starting the coffee and brushing out her hair, she bundled up in her coat, hat, scarf and gloves and scurried out into the early gray morning.

The temperature was below freezing, but nowhere near as bad as it had been the weekend before. There hadn't been a blizzard or even any actual snowfall, but the temperature had dropped below zero. Especially at night, it was dangerous to be out longer than absolutely necessary.

And Dottie's coat was old, worn, and even when new had not been the warmest.

She wanted to run for the paper, but the alley was a treacherous terrain of frozen puddles and even more treacherous patches of black ice. So she picked her way carefully out towards the sidewalk, snatched up the paper, then picked her way back to the office door.

Not so bad. She wouldn't have had a problem even if her scarf had slipped down from over her nose. But not a delight, either.

Dottie set the newspaper on the desk that was technically her brother's, although she was the one who spent most of her time sitting behind it. Then she hovered close to the radiator, holding out the sides of her coat like a tent to contain the warmth.

She didn't hear the outside door open and close behind her, even though she had left the door between the office and the corridor outside open. So she jumped at the sound of knuckles rapping briskly on the doorframe of the open door.

"Knock-knock?" a woman's voice called.

"We're not quite open yet," Dottie said. The coffee wasn't even ready yet. It was not quite seven, and the time posted on the door said eight.

But a client was a client, even if still only a potential one, so she kept her tone cheerful.

"I know. I'd say this a social call, but I'm afraid that would be fibbing a bit."

Dottie was smiling even before she turned to see her friend Evelyn Dawson standing in the doorway. She was dressed, as always, to the nines, in an elegant suit of deep green. Her shoes and her purse were of green leather and had matching patterns tooled into them, and her warm wool coat had an even warmer fur collar that snuggled around her neck up to her earlobes.

"You have a job for us?" Dottie asked as she hurried to hang her own coat and then Evelyn's on the coatrack by the door. "I hope it's not another troublesome family matter. Would you like some coffee?"

Evelyn glanced quickly at the coffee percolating on the little cooker behind Dottie, then quickly away again. "No, thank you, Dottie."

Dottie didn't blame her. She had probably finished a cup of the finest, freshest roasted coffee at home before venturing out to this decidedly less fashionable part of town. But she appreciated that Evelyn didn't say so.

"I'm afraid it may be a troublesome family matter, although thankfully mine is not the family in question," Evelyn went on as she smoothed her skirt before sitting on the chair positioned in front of the desk.

Dottie poured herself a cup of coffee before taking her own place behind the desk.

"Go on," she said, then blew the steam off the surface of the liquid before taking a small sip. Bitter, but not burnt. She would take it, and try not to wish too much for a little bit of cream. Their icebox upstairs was quite empty.

"The client is a friend of my father's. Another businessman. A property developer, actually. He is, especially by the standards of today, quite well off," Evelyn said.

Which was good news to Dottie. Lately, her brother had taken entirely too many jobs where they were paid in promises to return the favor someday. Promises didn't fill the icebox. Or pay the rent.

"And this is a family matter?" Dottie asked.

"Possibly," Evelyn said. "It is certainly a matter that the gentleman in question would like handled as discretely as possible. But he is not opposed to police involvement. No, the trouble came when he reported the crime to the police and they refused to take the case."

"Why?"

"They claim no crime was committed," Evelyn said with a hint of a smile.

"This certainly sounds interesting," Dottie said. "But I'm going to stop your story there for now. I have to go wake up John. Otherwise, you'll only end up telling it twice."

"I'll wait," Evelyn said, settling her pocketbook across her lap. But then she added with a look of sincere sympathy, "I do hope he wasn't up so very late."

"No, I don't believe so," Dottie said. But the truth was, she had no idea. Her corner of their apartment was only separated from the rest by a single curtain, but she was a very heavy sleeper. Even if her brother had come stumbling in drunk, which he would never do, she doubted it would wake her.

Her brother John, on the other hand, was not a heavy sleeper. So after she ran back up the stairs, the soles of her shoes tapping loudly in the enclosed space this time, it wasn't entirely surprising to find him sitting up in bed, blinking tiredly as he waited for her to appear in the doorframe.

"Case?" he grumbled as he scratched at his sleep-matted hair.

"An intriguing case, for a man who is rich

enough to pay," Dottie said. "Hurry down as quick as you can. Evelyn Dawson is waiting."

At the sound of that name, her brother snapped awake, throwing back his blanket and reaching for the clothes he had left on the chair the night before.

As quickly as he had been moving when she had been standing in the doorway, it still took several minutes for him to make his way down the stairs. But to judge by his appearance as he stepped into the office, he had put a little extra effort into washing up. His cheeks were still glowing red from the scrubbing, and he had transformed a chaotic mat of curls into a neatly combed-back style that was only showing a few signs of needing to be cut.

"Good morning, Miss Dawson," he said with a little nod before accepting the cup of coffee Dottie poured for him with a murmur of thanks. Then he sat in the desk chair as Dottie took her usual position leaning against the filing cabinet. From there she could both watch the entire conversation happening around the desk and soak in all the best warmth the radiator was casting off.

"Evelyn, please," Evelyn said to him. "You shared Thanksgiving with my family. Surely that puts us on a first name basis."

"Evelyn," John said, then cleared his throat before taking another sip of the scalding coffee. Then he took a pad of paper and a pencil out of the desk drawer and wrote the date and Evelyn's name on the top of the page. "All right. I'm ready."

"My father was called late last night by a friend of his, a man whose name you will certainly know, although I doubt your paths have ever crossed. George Hanson."

Dottie sucked in a breath, but her brother just nodded and wrote that name down on his paper.

But everyone in St. Paul knew the name of George Hanson. Not only was he a rich property developer, he had so many connections in the local government that the joke was he would actually have less power if he did what he always seemed on the verge of doing and actually ran for mayor.

He was also rumored to have mob connections as well. Although if he was as close to Evelyn's father as he seemed to be, she doubted that could possibly be true. Mr. Dawson had struck Dottie as a very honorable man.

"And what can we do for George Hanson?" John asked, looking up at Evelyn.

"And why did the police say it wasn't a case for them?" Dottie put in.

John shot a brief glance back at her over his shoulder, annoyed by her interruption. But he refrained from chastising her in front of her friend. And Dottie was used to ignoring those little looks, anyway.

"Mr. Hanson has a fondness for expensive automobiles. He has more than a dozen, most parked in the garage at his property on White Bear Lake. But a few of the choicest models he keeps in the carriage house on his property on Summit Avenue. Among those is his most recent acquisition, a Cadillac Series 65 convertible."

John nodded, scribbling more notes on his page than words Evelyn had spoken. He was already working on what his first steps would be, and they didn't even know what the crime was yet.

"Last Saturday, that convertible went missing. There was nothing in its spot in the carriage house but the cover that was meant to be over it during the winter months. But it was only missing for a day. By Sunday morning, it was back where it had been on Friday. The tank was full of gasoline, and the entire car was sparkling clean. Under the cover, of course. It was like nothing ever happened."

"So that's why the police refused to take the case?" John asked with a skeptical frown.

Evelyn just shrugged. "That was his story."

"Hm," John said, looking down at his notes as if the real answer laid there.

"What are you thinking?" Dottie asked.

"Mr. Hanson has children. Or rather, young adults?" John asked Evelyn.

"His son is away at Harvard, but his daughter still lives at home. She's nineteen," Evelyn said.

John glanced back at Dottie, speaking more to her than to Evelyn. "That's why they aren't involved, I'm guessing. They implied the list of suspects started with his own family, and he opted not to report the crime."

"Couldn't he just ask them, then?" Dottie asked.

"I know the one thing he specifically said to my father was that he knew you were quite discreet," Evelyn said. "He and my father are close enough that he is familiar with the circumstances of our long-lost cousin, and how you helped us out the two impostors."

"Do you know who found the car missing? Or who found the car when it was no longer missing? Or any other details?" John asked, glancing over his notes.

"I'm afraid not," Evelyn said. "But I did tell my father I would find a way to be sure you called on Mr. Hanson yourself just as early as possible. He is very anxious to know what happened to his beloved car."

"Of course. I can go at once," John said. Then he seemed to remember there was someone else in the room and turned to his sister. "You can watch the phones while I'm out?"

"I always do," Dottie said with her sweetest smile. As valuable to him as she'd been on so many occasions, he still preferred to believe that she was actively pursuing more suitable work. When, in fact, she had quite given up on that. He didn't want her to be a private investigator, but surely if she helped him grow his business, he wouldn't object to her being his secretary, receptionist and accountant all rolled into one?

Because she was already doing that, anyway. But it would be nice to make it official.

John put on his coat and hat and snatched up a pair of gloves before heading out the door. But Evelyn remained in the client chair in front of the desk, smiling at Dottie until she took the hint and slid into her brother's place.

"You have a theory?" Dottie asked and pulled out a pad of paper of her own. "I'm guessing you suspect the daughter."

"I don't know if I do, actually," Evelyn said.

"You know her pretty well, then?" Dottie asked.

"Mary Hanson? Only in passing. Enough to nod to at parties. She went to a much posher school than I did," Evelyn said. Then she blushed a little. She and Dottie had met at school, and any school that would've let in a policeman's daughter like Dottie was definitely not a posh one.

But then Dottie remembered that Evelyn hadn't wanted to go to a posher school. "Is Mary Hanson snooty?" she asked.

"Aloof, maybe," Evelyn said. "She's nineteen, so she's a bit younger than us. But her father is much richer, and she seems to place a lot of stock in the idea that that makes her my social superior. Maybe," she conceded again. "Maybe she thinks so. I'm not really sure. She could just be very shy, and she uses snootiness to cover for it."

"So she *is* snooty," Dottie said, dramatically making a note of that on her pad of paper just to make Evelyn laugh a little.

"I don't like to judge people," Evelyn said

after failing to cover her smile with her hand. Mostly because that smile danced in her eyes.

"Alas, that's my job," Dottie said. "Are you too distant for her to accept an invitation to tea?"

"Not too distant for me to try to extend one," Evelyn said. "But I don't know if she will accept."

"Can you try?" Dottie asked. "At the very least, living in the house where the crime took place, she might know something."

"I shall do my best," Evelyn said brightly.

Then she headed back to her own home up on Summit Avenue, leaving Dottie alone to ponder her mostly empty page of notes and cast frequent accusatory looks at the phone, which refused to ring.

It was nearly lunchtime before John returned. But the boredom of the morning hours was quickly forgotten when Dottie saw the bags of food her brother had brought in with him.

"Hot turkey sandwiches," he said as he set the bags of waxed paper on the desk. "And a couple of bottles of ginger ale."

"Are we celebrating?" Dottie asked as she hopped up to fetch plates from the cabinet by the cooker where they heated the coffee.

"Mr. Hanson did give us a very generous advance, so I guess we can call it a celebration," John said. He turned to hang up his coat, missing the pleased flush of pink that flooded his sister's cheeks when he said the word "us."

"An advance, so you didn't crack the case already?" Dottie asked as she unwrapped the still-hot sandwiches and arranged them on the plates.

"Not quite," John said. He dug around in his desk drawer for a bottle opener, then opened both of the ginger ales before settling down into his chair with the notepad he'd run out the door with hours before. Several pages were now full of notes.

"Tell me what you learned," Dottie said before biting into her sandwich. Turkey was her absolute favorite, and the diner around the corner where John had gotten the sandwiches baked their own crusty bread fresh every morning. This lunch was a rare treat, and she was determined to savor every bite.

But she also wanted to know what was on all those pages of notes.

"I think the car went to Chicago and back," John told her before taking a massive bite of his own sandwich. He had to keep a hand close to his mouth until he had chewed and swallowed it down, but then that hand started flipping through the pages of his pad. "More than eight hundred miles were put on the odometer between

Friday afternoon and Sunday morning. That's enough to get to Chicago and back for sure."

"What's in Chicago?" Dottie asked.

"That I don't know. Yet," John said with a frown. "But I spoke to Mr. Hanson's driver, an older man by the name of Harry Nelson. He's been working for Mr. Hanson for three decades now, and seems both content with his work and with his boss, as well as very meticulous in his job."

"He's the one who discovered the car was missing and then back again?" Dottie guessed.

"Yes, and he was the one who told me about the mileage," John said. "He keeps a record for each car, when he fuels them and how much and what the odometer reads each time. He had filled up the Cadillac Series 65 convertible in October just before it was parked and covered for the winter. He knows no one touched it since."

"How does he *know*?" Dottie interrupted to ask.

"When he isn't driving the boss around, he's in that garage," John said. "He starts his day there, and he ends it there. No one could've taken it for more than an hour or so at a time, but even then, with the snow we've had since October, he would've seen signs that the car had been moved.

Snowmelt on the garage floor, tracks in front of the door to that stall, that sort of thing."

"All right," Dottie said, and treated herself to another bite of sandwich. Then she asked, "What did you think of George Hanson?"

"I think he loves this car to perhaps an unhealthy extent," John said slowly, "but aside from that, he seems a perfect gentleman. He reminded me a lot of Mr. Dawson. I can see how they are close friends."

"Do you think he suspects someone in his family of taking his car?" Dottie asked. "It would make the most sense. It certainly seems like someone who knew the car was there just wanted to take it out for a spin, not to keep it."

"If it had been taken on a lovely June night, I might agree with you," John said. "But the coldest night in January is no time for a joyride in a convertible. And to answer your question, no, I don't think he suspects his family. But he was afraid that the police would question them, perhaps too aggressively. His family, and his staff as well. They've all been with him and his wife for decades. The newest hire was the nanny, and she's gone now that the children are grown. Everyone else has been there basically forever."

"They had steady employment through the

last few years when that was so rare," Dottie said. "I can see why they'd be loyal. Especially if he treats them well."

"It's possible the car was taken by any of a number of young people who knew it was there in the garage," John said with a sigh. "I tried to compile a list, but there were simply too many names. The Hansons host a great many parties, and attend an even larger amount. And Mr. Hanson freely admits he talks about his cars perhaps too zealously."

"Was there sign of a break-in?" Dottie asked.

"None that the driver Harry Nelson saw, and I believe if there'd been any, he would've seen it. You should've heard him go on about the tracks he would've noticed in the snow if the car had been moved since October," John said with a fond smile. "I do believe if a single fly had landed on that canvas-covered automobile, he would've sensed it. Like a spider senses a fly caught in their web."

"The number of miles is enough to get to Chicago and back, but that isn't much to go on," Dottie said. "Maybe they took a circuitous route to Duluth or Des Moines or Milwaukee. They might not even have gone further than Chippewa Falls if they spent a great deal of time just driving up and down the main roads here or there."

"Maybe," John said. But he didn't sound like he believed it.

"You said it was probably young people who stole it," Dottie said.

"Maybe," he said again. Then he put the last of his sandwich in his mouth, chewing before washing it down with the last of the ginger ale. "But anyway, Mr. Hanson gave me this advance because he agreed I should go to Chicago to look for another lead."

"Chicago?" Dottie repeated. "That's so far away."

"I'll be back tomorrow," he said with a shrug.

"You'll be back tomorrow if you find something right away," she said. "But how could you? You don't even know what you're looking for."

"It's a distinctive car," John said. "If people saw it, they would remember it."

Dottie bit her lip. She knew too many people who didn't have any interest in cars to have the same faith her brother did that anyone would remember this one in particular. Even though it was a convertible driving around in the dead of winter. Even then.

There were simply too many people who

didn't notice much of anything at all. Particularly when it was bone-chilling cold.

And the Saturday night it had been missing had been the coldest of the winter so far. Who would even have been out?

And what were John's chances of stumbling upon them again if they had?

But she didn't try to talk him out of it. If he had already interviewed the driver and the staff, as well as Mr. Hanson himself, and had examined the returned car as thoroughly as she knew he must have done, going to Chicago was really the next step for him in the investigation.

Dottie, meanwhile, had other avenues to explore.

John left shortly after lunch, promising to call as soon as he arrived in Chicago, sooner if the old car they'd inherited from their father had a breakdown somewhere in Wisconsin. He further promised that the advance he'd gotten in cash was more than enough to pay for any tow truck or road service he might need.

And then he was gone, and she was alone.

She picked up the phone and called Evelyn Dawson.

Three hours later, Dottie was in Evelyn Dawson's lovely sitting room, perched on the edge of a chair that looked like she'd break it to pieces if she slumped back into it. Not that Dottie was a large woman. Few were these days; the Depression had made keeping a slender figure all too easy.

But the thought of that delicate chair beneath her certainly made it easier not to dive into the platter of tea cakes when the maid brought them in.

Evelyn took one and set it on her plate, licking a crumb of sugary crust off of her thumb, but otherwise not touching the cake itself. The tea was ready, but she left it in the pot wrapped snuggly in a cozy, waiting for the arrival of their tardy guest.

"Mary Hanson said no, then?" Dottie asked, mostly to fill the silence that was otherwise being dominated by the ticking of the clock on the fireplace mantel.

"Her maid said she wasn't feeling up for going out," Evelyn said.

"So she's ill?" Dottie asked. That could be a clue.

But Evelyn was smiling as she shook her head. "No, it just means she doesn't want to be too rude about turning down my invitation. Having the maid refuse for her over the phone is about what I could expect, really. As I've told you, we're not really close."

"But you are close with this woman who is coming?" Dottie asked.

"Actually, I don't know Margaret Anderson at all," Evelyn said airily. "But her family is not quite so rich as the Hansons. So she answers her own phone. And she was intrigued enough to meet us. Or so she said," she added with a glance at that loud clock behind her.

"But she's Mary Hanson's closest friend?" Dottie asked.

"No, I believe that's Ruth Miller," Evelyn said with a little frown. "But Ruth, I couldn't get ahold of at all. Apparently, no one has seen her for days. Her family was quite upset about it. When I rang, her mother snatched the phone from the maid. I guess there was some confusion, she thought from what she overheard that I was Ruth herself calling home. She didn't take it well when I admitted not only was I not Ruth, but I had no idea where Ruth was."

"Curiouser and curiouser," Dottie said.

Then they heard the sound of the butler opening the front door, followed by the murmur of voices, one of them distinctly feminine. Footsteps approached the sitting room doors, then the butler opened the double doors to announce, "Miss Margaret Anderson to see you, Miss Evelyn."

"Thank you," Evelyn said as she and Dottie both got to their feet to receive their guest.

The butler bowed his head, then stepped aside, leaving the woman behind him standing awkwardly alone, twisting the pocketbook in her hands in a way that was sure to bruise the leather. She looked to be about nineteen, probably a classmate of Mary Hanson's. And the elegance of her clothing and the dressing of her hair were very much in keeping with someone who had gone to the poshest of finishing schools. Her skirt length was the exact specification of the latest fashions, her shoes hinted that they had come from Paris, and her hair was almost too natural a shade of blonde. At any rate, no one's hair was so perfectly uniform in shade, in Dottie's experience.

She also looked like she hadn't slept in days. Her makeup might be expertly applied, but it didn't quite cover the dark circles under her eyes.

Just like the polite smile she offered them didn't take away from the sense that she was on the verge of tears, and had been for some time.

"Miss Anderson, thank you so much for coming," Evelyn said, moving across the room to put an arm around Margaret's shoulders and guide her to the couch. Maybe too familiar a touch for acquaintances, but Margaret didn't object.

"Tea?" Dottie asked as she bent over the teapot to slip off the quilted cozy.

"Yes, thank you," Margaret said, looking from Evelyn to Dottie, then back again, as if she really didn't know which of the two of them she was thanking. Dottie poured a cup for her, added a few lumps of sugar, then gave it a stir before placing it directly in Margaret's hands.

Margaret murmured another thanks, then took a larger than entirely polite sip of tea. But it seemed to rejuvenate her, and she took another before letting the tension ease out of her body. Then she gave them both a slightly less tentative smile. "Miss Dawson, I know you at least a little from parties we've both been invited to. But I'm afraid I don't know you at all?" She gave Dottie a concerned frown.

"This is Dorothy Lundegaard," Evelyn said, her arm still around Margaret's shoulders. "She is my dearest friend, and you can trust her implicitly."

"Pleased to meet you, Miss Anderson," Dottie said. "But call me Dottie, please."

"Dottie," she said with a nod and a smile. "Call me Margaret, then."

"And I'm Evelyn," Evelyn concluded with a brighter smile, giving Margaret's shoulders a squeeze before moving over to her own chair and taking up the cup of tea Dottie had just poured out for her.

"I'm afraid I was a little out of sorts when you reached me by phone," Margaret said. "You had questions about Ruth, was it?" Then she took another sip of tea, but with the air of someone who needed a gesture to cover up an emotional response.

Dottie pretended to sip at her own tea, but was watching Margaret very closely. The young woman seemed to be hiding something. And if she was hiding something, Dottie wanted to be watching for signs of what she reacted to. It was a surer path to the truth than a straightforward question that would be left unanswered.

"Mary Hanson, actually," Evelyn said to Margaret and took a small nibble off of her tea cake.

Dottie's close attention was instantly rewarded, as the color washed out of Margaret's face entirely. Which was saying something, that she looked pale even with all the makeup working so hard to give her rosy color.

"Why would you want to ask me anything about Mary Hanson?" Margaret asked, licking her lips nervously. "I mean, Ruth is the one who is missing."

"Is she?" Evelyn asked coyly.

Dottie hastily wiped at her mouth with her napkin lest Margaret see the smile she couldn't quite repress. But Evelyn always made it so much easier for Dottie to do her job. She just had a way of putting people at ease and getting them talking. Dottie could do the same with ordinary people, but when it came to the sorts of girls who had made her school years such a torment, she never had any luck creating a rapport.

"I thought you knew that," Margaret said. Her growing confusion was increasing her distress, so much so that she set her teacup and saucer on the table. But the sound of the china clattering against each other in her shaking hands had already been noted by Dottie and likely Evelyn both.

"I know her mother is quite upset," Evelyn said. "I called her just before I called you."

"You did? What did you tell her?" Margaret asked, sitting forward on the edge of the couch.

Dottie supposed this was in case she felt the urge to bolt out of the room, but she couldn't erase the mental image of Margaret being as worried about the sturdy couch collapsing beneath her as Dottie herself was about the spindly chair she was sitting on.

"All I told her was that I wasn't Ruth, and I didn't know what happened to Ruth," Evelyn said.

"Oh," Margaret said. She thought this information over carefully. Then she pushed back on the couch, as if forcing herself to relax. But her body was still taut, her back too rigid with tension to even touch the pillows behind her.

"Mary's maid told me she was feeling under the weather," Evelyn said. "Is that because of Ruth, do you think?"

"Maybe," Margaret said, but there was a vague sound to her voice, like she wasn't really listening to the question when she answered it.

"She must be worried about her. They're quite close, aren't they?" Evelyn went on.

"We're all close," Margaret said. But still with that same distracted tone to her voice.

Dottie chewed at her lip as she studied the blonde woman across from her. She was clearly worried to distraction about something. But despite the fact that her friend Ruth Miller was missing, it was Mary's name that had put her close to panic.

In a rush of inspiration, Dottie found herself saying, "Does Mary have any friends in Chicago, by any chance?"

Evelyn gave her a puzzled frown, but then again, Dottie hadn't told her yet about what few clues John had been able to find that morning at the Hanson house. Dottie shot her a quick look begging her not to ask any questions about it just yet, then turned her attention back to Margaret.

Who was pale again, at the edge of panic.

"Chicago? Why would she have friends in Chicago? We all went to school here in town," Margaret said. "A few of the girls have gone to Manhattan in search of husbands, but most of us have stayed right here."

"Perhaps a cousin, then?" Dottie said casually, as if she hadn't even noticed how agitated Margaret was getting.

Which only agitated Margaret further.

"No, no cousins. Not that I know of. What are these questions?" Margaret asked. She turned to look at Evelyn, who was in the middle of sipping from her teacup.

Evelyn set the cup and saucer down, then wiped nothing Dottie could see from her lips with her napkin before folding her hands over her knee and turning towards Margaret to answer. "I'm sorry, Margaret. I should really explain. My friend Dottie here is a private investigator."

"A private investigator?" Margaret repeated.

"Actually, my brother is the private investigator," Dottie said. "But he's in Chicago at the moment, so I'm asking a few questions to see what I can learn before he gets back."

"Your brother is in Chicago?" Margaret said, putting her hands to her temples and rubbing them as if hoping to ward off a growing headache. "Your brother, a private investigator, is in Chicago right now?"

"Yes," Dottie said. "You seem quite upset about that. Is there something you want to tell me?"

"Mary Hanson isn't in Chicago," Margaret said. "He's not going to find her there."

"No, we know she's home," Dottie said. Evelyn gave her a questioning look, but Dottie just gave her a firm nod. Her brother would've seen everyone in the flesh when he was at the house. If he hadn't, that information would've been in his notebook, and he would've told her when they'd been eating those turkey sandwiches.

Mary Hanson most definitely wasn't in Chicago.

Ruth Miller, on the other hand...

"The car is back where it should be," Evelyn said. "So you don't have to worry about that."

"The car," Margaret said, as if the word had no meaning for her. Then something clicked. She dropped her hands and looked directly at Dottie. "Someone noticed the car was gone?"

"Mr. Hanson noticed the car was gone," Dottie said, and Margaret blanched yet again. "After his driver noticed it, I should say," Dottie added.

"We were so sure he wouldn't," Margaret said, rubbing at her temples again.

"Who is 'we,' dear?" Evelyn asked her as she slid to the very edge of her chair so she could rest a hand on Margaret's knee.

"Mary, Ruth and I," Margaret said. "We didn't steal the car, I swear it. We only borrowed it."

"Without asking for Mr. Hanson's permission," Dottie said.

"I know. Mary was sure he wouldn't notice. He was supposed to be in New York, you know. From Thursday until next Saturday. On business. But I guess that was cancelled. But it was too late.

We had to go through with the plan, anyway. But Mary was sure he would never notice. Because it was January. He wasn't going to want to take the car out at all in January."

"No, he didn't want to take it out. But he was very protective of it. Was that really the best choice for whatever you were planning?" Dottie asked.

"I argued against it, but Mary was firm," Margaret said. Dottie guessed there'd been an argument, to judge by the rush of red color to Margaret's cheeks at the memory she was recounting. Still, it was good to see the color coming back to her pale face.

"She wanted to take the convertible out for a spin?" Evelyn asked.

"Not like that," Margaret said. "No, she said that if anyone knew we were going, they would be very careful indeed not to damage that car trying to force Ruth to come home. Even the…the sorts of people we were helping Ruth run away from," she ended lamely.

"Gangsters," Dottie guessed.

"Maybe," Margaret said. "I mean, Prohibition has been over for years."

"And yet organized crime remains," Dottie said.

"Albeit in a weakened state, if the might of someone like George Hanson is enough to quell them," Evelyn said.

"It's just what Mary said," Margaret mumbled. "She maybe thinks too much of her father. But I guess she was right, because we took that car and drove through the night until we got to Chicago. And then we drove back again. And I know suspicious cars definitely spotted us when we were leaving and when we were returning both. But no one stopped us."

"Maybe they didn't care that much about Ruth," Evelyn suggested.

Margaret tried to speak. Then she swallowed hard and tried again. On the third try, she managed to say, "Her fiancé William Schmidt knocked out three of her teeth when she told him she wanted to call off the wedding. All she did was say the words, and he hit her that hard. I guess we knew what would happen to her if he caught her actually trying to get away from him. And it wouldn't be pretty."

"Ruth is in Chicago now?" Dottie asked.

"She is," Margaret said. "She's staying with a cousin of mine. It was as far removed from her own connections as we could get her."

"It's likely not far enough," Evelyn said grimly.

"No," Margaret readily admitted. "We're trying to get her to Europe. She'll be safe in Europe."

Dottie and Evelyn traded a glance. They both hoped Margaret was right about that. But neither was quite so confident.

"I need to get back to the office," Dottie said, and Margaret looked up at her in real alarm. "I need to be there when my brother calls. To tell him to stop looking for…anything at all."

"You would do that?" Margaret asked, her voice little more than a breath of sound.

"I will," Dottie said. But then she had to add, "We'll have to tell Mr. Hanson what happened to his car. We signed a contract with him to find that out, and we can't back out of it now. Mary will have to take whatever punishment he deems fit."

"I understand," Margaret said. "Mary will too. We only wanted to delay as long as we could, or she would've confessed sooner."

"Is Ruth still in Chicago?" Evelyn asked.

"She is," Margaret said, close to tears now. "We've been trying to raise money among her friends to get her a train ticket and passage on a ship, to keep her moving away from William

Schmidt, but everyone we know only has access to so much funds. And our fathers monitor our spending so closely."

Dottie wondered what that life was like. But only briefly. In this case, it sounded like a lot of wealthy young women were doing everything they could to put that wealth to good use.

And were feeling pretty frustrated that it simply wasn't enough.

"My brother won't reach Chicago until late tonight," Dottie said. "And it will take him until tomorrow afternoon to get back again. That gives you a little more time. I'm sorry we can't give you more."

"No, you've already done enough," Margaret said.

Dottie didn't feel like that was quite true. But she didn't know what more was within the realm of possibility for her.

Three short winter days later found Dottie back in her brother's office, leaning against the filing cabinet as her brother explained the whole story to George Hanson.

George Hanson wasn't as tall as she had been

expecting. And there was more gray in his hair than showed up in newspaper photographs.

But he also looked far kinder, the lines on his face shifting from expressions of annoyance at his daughter to deep concern as John told him the sadder parts of the tale.

"I never liked that William Schmidt," Mr. Hanson said, pressing a tight fist close to his cheekbone as if feeling acutely the futility of the desire to strike at someone not in the room. "His father is a man of few uses, but somehow came out of Prohibition with funds no one could possibly have legally acquired. But his son? Less than useless."

"I do gather that Miss Ruth Miller is well shut of him," John said with his usual ease of diplomacy. His job may be to investigate people, but unlike Dottie, he didn't think that meant judging them.

Dottie just wished that this William Schmidt fellow was there, so Mr. Hanson could take that punch at him.

But that was not to be.

And it wasn't like she could do it herself.

But Mr. Hanson let out a sigh, then slumped back in his chair. "She is still in Chicago? Miss Miller?"

"We believe so," John said. Dottie recognized that hedging tone in his voice, although she would bet it was too subtle for Mr. Hanson to pick up on. But her brother was definitely getting nervous about what was going to happen next.

"And you have a way of getting word to her?" Mr. Hanson asked.

"Not myself personally," John said.

Now he was hedging so clearly that even Mr. Hanson could see it. The man slammed his hands down on the arms of his chair with such a slap both Lundegaards jumped.

"Damn it, man! Do you have a means to get funds to her or not?"

"Funds, sir?" John asked.

"Of course, funds," Mr. Hanson said. "You just told me she's trying to get to Europe. But that alone will not see her safe. Her family was too anxious for this attachment to the Schmidt family. I fear they will betray her, if given the chance. No, Miss Miller needs money for a train ticket to the coast, and passage on a ship to Europe, and funds to start a life there. But she will also need aid in acquiring a new name. Anonymity. It's her best hope."

"And you're looking to give it to her?" John

asked, trying hard not to sound as incredulous as Dottie knew he felt. Because she felt it too.

"I am," Mr. Hanson said. "I'll double your rate if you can assist me in this manner."

"No need, no need," John said, waving his hands as he refused the extra money.

"She is staying with a cousin of Margaret Anderson's," Dottie said. "Your daughter Mary knows her. The two of them can get all of your assistance to her."

"Mary," Mr. Hanson said, with an edge to his voice. Like he'd just remembered why he was there in the first place.

Because his daughter had stolen his most beloved car. And had tried to cover that theft up.

But then his face softened again. "Mary did all this to help a friend. I..." he started to say, but then tears started forming in the corners of his eyes. He brushed them away almost aggressively before saying, "I've misjudged her. Terribly. It's my own fault she kept things from me. But I never thought she would do so much, risk so much, for a friend."

"She must be very loyal," Dottie said.

"More than I knew," he said. But then he gave himself a shake and was once more all business. "I do thank you for your help in this. I will have to tell Dawson he did not oversell you. I was sure he had."

"Thank you," John said, blinking at the compliment that skirted so close to not being a compliment.

And then he was gone.

"I know what you're thinking," John said, although his gaze was still fixed on the desk in front of him and not on his sister standing behind him.

"If you're going to say that I think you should've taken that money, you're wrong," she said.

He turned to look at her with frank surprise.

"I mean, money is nice. And we definitely need more of it. But I don't want to get paid extra for doing the right thing any more than you do. We're Lundegaards. We don't do that," she said.

"That's right," he said with a growing grin on his face. "We're Lundegaards."

Dottie just smiled back at him.

But it was nice, anytime he said "we."

The sign over the office did say Lundegaard Investigations, after all. And someday, that was going to mean both of them.

DUMBER THAN DIRT

LIBBY FISCHER HELLMANN

Derek's father used to call him dumber than dirt. His mother said he wasn't the sharpest knife in the dishwasher. Both of them said he had more luck than brains. Like the time he accidentally shoved the gearshift in reverse and backed his father's '78 Dodge Challenger into a wall. No one got hurt, but eight-year-old Derek felt his sore bottom for days. He felt something else, too. He'd only gripped the wheel for a few seconds, but the thrust of the engine was so powerful, his sense of control so profound, that Derek was hooked on cars.

As he grew up, his passion deepened. He didn't care much about the engineering. Or the technology. But the cold sleek lines of a classic design, the supple leather of a bucket seat, the hum of a perfectly tuned engine triggered an urgent need in him—a need that could only be met by flooring it every chance he got. He spent his high-school years happily scouting, admiring, and borrowing the objects of his desire, sometimes without the owner's permission. But Derek never thought too much about the consequences of his actions, and while his friends went off to college, Derek went off to East Moline for two to five. He swore afterwards he'd never be seduced by a V-8's siren song again.

That summer he got a job at Lindsey's, a pub on Chicago's north side. Lindsey's sported lots of polished oak, soft lights, and a dartboard in back. They served tiny steaks with blue cheese on top, and the place was always crowded. Chuck Lindsey was a Sixties liberal who thought everyone deserved a second chance. He hired Derek to wash dishes and sweep floors. Derek found a room a few blocks away and walked to work. In Lakeview most folks did, and the dearth of cars helped Derek avoid temptation. He cheerfully joined the throngs of pedestrians hoofing it down the street, another skinny young man with long hair and a slightly sleepy expression.

He was on the early shift one morning, rinsing out pots, when he heard a knock at the door. He walked out to the front and squinted through the window. It was Brady, a regular who sat with Lindsey almost every night, sharing jokes and stories and drinks. The bus boys said Brady threw money around like water. Once in a while Brady's wife, a hot blond number, came in. Today, though, Brady wasn't smiling. As Derek opened the door, he felt waves of tension eddying out from Brady.

"Lindsey in back?" *No "hello, how are you, pal."* Brady never looked at you when he spoke, as if people were annoying, things you swatted away like flies.

"He's not here."

"He must be." Brady sounded irritated, as if it was Derek's fault, and brushed past him. Derek started sweeping. Last night, he was loading the dishwasher when he heard loud voices coming from Lindsey's cramped office next to the kitchen. Then there'd been silence. A few minutes later Derek saw Brady slink down the hall, his face half-hidden by a baseball cap pulled low across his forehead.

Now, Brady pushed past him again. "You hear from him this morning?"

Derek shrugged. "Nope."

Brady opened the door. "When he comes in, have him call me." Not a request. An order.

"Sure thing, Mr. Brady." The door slammed.

A few minutes later, Derek caught a gleam of silver wedged between a barstool and the foot rail. Thinking it was a gum wrapper, he leaned over to pick it up. It was a set of car keys. A small tag asked the finder to return them to Ian Brady at a post office number. Derek turned them over in his hand. One key was silver, but the other was that new kind of key that wasn't a key at all, just a finger of black plastic. Mercedes made them.

Derek laid the keys on the bar. Brady would be charging back in as soon as he realized he'd dropped them.

He finished sweeping the floor. Then he unloaded the dishwasher. Half an hour passed. Brady wasn't back. Derek started to itch all over. He stayed in the kitchen and tried not to think about the keys. Twenty minutes later the itch was still there, and his face felt hot. He checked the clock. Lindsey would be in any minute, along with the lunchtime crew.

He walked back to the bar. The keys glinted in a shaft of sunlight. He ran his thumb and forefinger around his jaw-line, stroking an imaginary beard, a habit he'd picked up that made him feel smart. He stared at the keys. Then he scooped them up and let himself out the door.

The Benz couldn't be too far away. Derek walked up one block and down another. No car. Puzzled, he doubled back through the alley behind the restaurant. There it was, parked in the spot Lindsey usually kept vacant for suppliers. A navy blue coupe that looked like it just came off the showroom floor. Cream interior. Deep pile carpeting. Fat seventeen inch tires. It had to be over five hundred horsepower. That thing would fly.

He skulked in the narrow shadow from an overhanging eave, his eyes scanning the buildings across the alley. This was the hottest summer since the year all those people died, and today was already a scorcher. Everyone must be holed up next to their air conditioners with the blinds down. Derek sauntered up to the car and pressed the dot of raised plastic on the key. The locks snapped up. He swung himself into the car. The leather seat yielded to the contours of his back, as though it was custom tailored for him. He gripped the wheel and turned over the engine. It caught right away. He nudged the car out of the alley.

Heading east to the Drive, he handled the Benz as gently as one of Lindsey's crystal glasses, the ones he saved for special occasions. The slightest touch of his hand prompted an eager response, as if the car was anxious for his next command. The ride was well balanced and stable, and it cornered on a matchstick. He cruised down the Drive, getting the feel of the car, then turned south on Fifty-Five.

The road opened up a few miles later, and Derek floored it. The car hesitated for a fraction of a second, then lunged forward. Derek hunched forward and let the car eat up the highway. There was always a moment when he could tell whether a set of wheels was worth it or whether it had some defect, some flaw that made it a clunker. But this baby was perfect. Derek blew out his breath. It felt like he hadn't really breathed in years. His fingers drifted over the walnut-trimmed instrument panel, the velvety smoothness of the seats. He wasn't sure where the car ended and his flesh began.

When Derek smelled it, he thought it might be fertilizer from a nearby field until he spotted the warehouses flanking the highway. Then he popped open the glove compartment, thinking Brady left a burger or hot dog inside. He found lipstick, tissues, and a garage door opener, but no food.

The odor grew more rancid, and he opened the windows. That helped for a while, but when he closed them to crank up the A/C, it came back. An uneasy feeling twisted his stomach. He veered off the highway at the next exit and stopped. The smell was strongest near the trunk. He got out and opened it up.

He jumped back as if he'd singed his fingers on the trunk. He took a cautious step forward.

The body of a man was curled up inside. There were brown stains all over his khaki pants and polo shirt. On his feet were black Converses, the kind Lindsey wore. The hair on the back of Derek's neck stiffened. It *was* Lindsey.

The sudden roar of a passing car reminded Derek the trunk was wide open. He pushed it down. His pulse raced. This had to be a bad dream. If he opened the trunk again, it would be empty.

He did. It wasn't.

He glimpsed a patch of red plastic peeking out from under Lindsey's body. He pulled it out. It was a shopping bag from one of those fancy Lakeview stores. Inside was a crumpled white shirt with the same brown stains, and a large butcher's knife, it too stained with blood. Derek froze. The knife was from the restaurant's kitchen.

He stiffened. He had a big problem, and grand theft auto was just the beginning. A minute passed. He walked up to the passenger side and pulled the tissues out of the glove compartment. He edged around to the back and slid the knife out of the bag, using the tissues to keep his prints off. Clutching the knife, he jogged to a wooded area set back from the road, found a patch of dead leaves and twigs, and buried the knife underneath.

Seconds later, he was back behind the wheel heading south on Fifty-Five. Calmer now, he turned on the radio and twisted the dial to a country station. Tim McGraw was singing *I Like It, I Love It*. Derek thumped the wheel to the beat. Then he noticed the cell phone built into Brady's car. His hand flew to his chin and stroked it for a moment. He punched in a number.

"Louie? It's Derek." Louie was from East Moline. They'd worked in the laundry together, listening to country all day long. It was Louie who told him who was married to Faith Hill.

"Derek, my man. Still keeping your ass clean?" Louie guffawed. He knew Derek was a dishwasher.

"Louie, I got a problem."

"Hold on, lemme get to another phone."

Derek heard a shrill voice in the background. "You already had one lousy break today. This better not take long."

"Don't mess with me, woman," Louie's voice snapped. Then he was back. "What's happening, man?"

Derek told him. There was a long silence.

"Where are you now?"

"In the car."

"Man, are you crazy? You calling me from

some dude's car? What's the matter with you? Get to a pay phone and call me back." There was a click and the line went dead.

Derek drove to the nearest gas station, but a few people were filling up their tanks, and he couldn't risk someone getting a whiff of Lindsey. He sailed past it then redialed Louie's number.

"You at a pay phone?"

"Er, yeah, Louie."

"It don't sound like it."

Derek took a breath. "Louie, I don't know what to do."

"Only one thing to do. Get your ass out of that car. Fast. Dump it."

"Can you help me?"

"No way, man. Ditching cars is one thing. Dead bodies is somethin' altogether different. Screw it man. You shouldna' called me."

"Louie, don't hang up. Please."

More silence.

"Louie?"

"Yeah?"

"Where do I dump it?"

"Anywhere man. Just do it." Louie sounded impatient. "Shit. You got no clue, do you?"

Derek shook his head, not realizing Louie couldn't see him.

"All right. Listen to me good now, Derek. You remember that movie we saw in the joint?"

"What movie?" Derek loved movies. When he could follow the plot.

"Think. The one about Bernie. You remember?"

Derek thought hard, his lips pursed together with the effort. It was something about two guys trying to figure out what to do with a dead body. *Weekend At Bernie's*. "Yeah." He was proud of himself. "I remember."

"Well, where's the one place we thought they shoulda' ditched him, but they didn't?"

Derek thought he recalled some of the guys acting like they knew all about dumping stiffs, but he couldn't remember what they said. "I—I dunno."

"Man, do I have to spell it out for you?"

Derek hung his head.

"Listen. I'm not gonna say it straight out—you never know who's listening. But you get yerself out to the airport, you hear?"

The muscles on his face relaxed. "I got it. Thanks, Louie."

"And we never talked, you got it?"

"Sure."

"Derek?"

"Yeah, Louie?"

"Long term parking."

"Right."

Derek cut northeast towards O'Hare. He might catch on slow, but he knew what to do now. He'd ditch the Mercedes then race into the airport like he was boarding a plane. Then he'd make a one-eighty and take the subway home. His problems would be over. He turned up the radio and whistled along with Garth Brooks.

But when he got to long term parking, he realized they'd just finished renovating the lots. There was now a booth next to the automatic gate, and inside sat a black man, or Double-A as Louie called them. Derek pulled up and waited for his ticket.

The man stared at Derek with narrowed eyes, and Derek felt a jolt of recognition. The guy was an ex-con. Louie said you could always tell. There was something in the eyes, something that marked you as a former inmate, and it never went away, no matter how long you were out. Derek realized he should have waited until dark. The booth might have been empty, or even if someone *was* there, they'd probably be jammin' to the music from their headphones, taking no notice of a guy in a Benz. He circled the lot and pretended to change his mind. As he looped back to the highway, he felt the guy staring after him.

Derek cruised through neighborhoods where the same house reproduced itself in different hues of paint. After an hour or so he came to an industrial area dotted with warehouses and factories. He sat up straighter. The road dead-ended just ahead. Beyond it was a field, waist high with prairie grass. Nothing else. He stopped and got out of the car. There was no traffic. Or people. He was about to toss the keys into the field and run like hell when he heard a voice behind him.

"Nice wheels, man."

Derek whipped around. A kid on a bike. The kid braked to a stop.

"A Cl600 with a V-12 engine, right?"

Derek didn't know what model it was, but he dipped his head anyway.

"I know a guy has one of those new CLK350s, but this baby is wicked sweet."

Derek grunted. The kid went on about independent suspension, torque, and power transmissions, clearly trying to impress Derek with his knowledge. But Derek didn't want to shoot the breeze. He had to split before the kid smelled Lindsey.

"What are you doing around here, anyway?" The kid wrinkled his nose.

Derek's stomach flipped. He shrugged, struggling to act nonchalant. What should he say? Luckily, the kid gave him an out.

"You work around here?"

"Yeah," Derek said, almost grateful. "Yeah. I do."

"Oh. You must have just started, right? 'Cause I never seen your car before."

Derek nodded. Then a thought came to him. "You know what time it is?"

The kid shook his head.

"I gotta go. They dock you an hour's pay if you take too long on break."

He got back in the car and tried not to lay down any rubber as he pulled away.

By late afternoon, the stench from the trunk was turning his skin clammy. Blasting the A/C didn't help, and the hot angry air whipping through the window scalded his arm. He sped up Ninety-Four to Milwaukee, then backtracked south. He'd missed his shift; he hoped Lindsey wouldn't fire him. Then he giggled. Lindsey wouldn't be firing anyone anymore. By nightfall, though, he was drained. He was a prisoner in the Benz, just as surely as he'd been in the joint. He was hungry and tired, and he didn't know what to do.

It wasn't until three in the morning, occasional headlights winking past him on the Skyway, that he had an epiphany. This wasn't his problem. It was Brady's. Brady killed Lindsey. He, Derek, was guilty of only one thing: taking the car for a joyride. If he could somehow undo that, he'd be in the clear. He played with the idea, turning it over in his mind, like a new car you want to baby until you know its limits.

The sun was just breaking over Lincoln Park, streaking the sky with pink when Derek drove east on Fullerton. He found Brady's home easily—his address was in the glove compartment. It was a neat brick townhouse, surrounded by a wrought iron fence in front and a small garage on the side. A discreet sign mounted on the gate asked visitors to announce themselves. He parked the car, got out, and left the keys in the ignition. He pressed the buzzer and then sprinted to the corner where he crouched behind a shuttered newsstand and peeked out.

Brady's door opened; Brady and his wife emerged. Brady's wife was in a bathrobe, her blond hair in tangles, but Brady was wearing the same clothes he'd worn yesterday. Both of them looked shocked to see the Benz. His wife waved her arms in the air, then pointed a finger at Brady. Brady's arms flew up as if he thought she might hit him. Then he gestured to the house and hurried inside.

His wife waited until the front door closed. Then she strolled up to the driver's side, looked in both directions, and took the keys out of the ignition. Back at the trunk, she inserted the key and raised the hood. Ten seconds passed. Then Derek heard her scream, loud enough to carry a full block away. She slammed down the trunk and ran up the driveway, clutching her stomach with her hands. Derek thought she was going to throw up. He waited until he heard the sirens approaching before he left. He thought he might have forgotten something, but he didn't know what it was.

Derek couldn't decide whether to show up for work. If he didn't, someone would wonder where he was, but if he did, they'd ask where he'd been yesterday. He decided to go in and say he'd been sick. He needed the money.

The sign said Lindsey's was closed, but the

place was crawling with cops. A couple of uniforms shielded the door. When he told them his name, they said to duck under the yellow tape stretched across the front. A man in a fancy suit and silk tie stood at the bar, talking into a cell phone. His skin was the shade of cocoa, his nappy black hair grizzled at the sides. His eyes were fearless.

"I know, but it's the closest thing we got to a crime scene." His eyes locked on Derek trying to slip through the door. "This is the last place anyone saw him alive." The man pointed to a table. Derek sat down. A guy taking pictures was just finishing up, while another guy started to smear black powder all over everything. "Call me back when you have something." The man who'd been talking snapped the phone closed and dumped it in his jacket pocket.

"Luke Woolston. Area Three Detectives." The man nodded to Derek. "Who are you?"

Derek stammered. "D-Derek Schroeder."

"They told me you missed work yesterday."

"Yeah." Derek refused to meet the detective's eyes.

Woolston took a swizzle stick off the bar, stuck it in his mouth. "How come?"

Derek gazed past the detective. The guy with

the briefcase was dusting the top of the bar with white powder. "I got no A/C. I couldn't breathe."

Woolston twirled the swizzle stick in his mouth. "You go to the ER? See a doctor?"

Derek shook his head.

"But you made a miraculous recovery." The detective curled his lip.

"I took lots of showers."

Woolston sat down across from Derek. "When was your last shift?"

"Yesterday morning."

"Where did you go afterwards?"

"Home."

The detective's cell phone rang. Woolston pulled it out of his pocket. "Good. Keep on it." He laid the phone on the table, his eyes never leaving Derek's face. "We've got a problem."

Derek looked at the cell phone.

"Yesterday we got a report of a stolen Mercedes. Brand new car. Then, less than twenty-four hours later, the car shows up. With Mr. Lindsey in the trunk." He took the swizzle stick out of his mouth and pointed to the phone. "Now, I hear you did two to five for stealing cars."

Derek blinked.

"You see the problem?" Woolston twirled the swizzle stick. "Let me try out a theory on you, son." He stood up, walked around to Derek, laid a hand on the back of Derek's chair. Derek had to twist around to see him. "I'm prepared to believe that whoever killed Lindsey didn't intend to kill him. I think the offender—" Woolston took his time with each syllable—"was just out for a joyride. And you know, I can understand that."

Derek cocked his head.

"I was into cars myself," Woolston smiled. "I was runnin' a 327 in a Fifty-Four Bel Air. Nothing like the feel of a Hurst shift in your hands, you know? Course that was a while back."

Derek felt his lips curve up in a smile.

"So," Woolston went on, "Lindsey might have seen this person in the act of—shall we say—liberating—Brady's car. And the person panicked. He knew he'd be sent back inside. So he did the only thing he could think of. He stabbed Lindsey with a knife." Woolston wandered back to his own chair. His eyes gave away nothing. "What do you think of that theory, Derek?"

Derek's foot started tapping the floor under the table. He tried to stop; he knew it didn't look good. He couldn't.

"You come down to station with me, son. You can tell me all about it."

"Brady and Lindsey had a fight," Derek blurted out.

Woolston raised an eyebrow.

"Two nights ago. I was loading the dishwasher. Lindsey's office is right next to the kitchen. I see Brady comin' out of the office. All sneaky like. Then, when I'm on the early shift yesterday morning, he shows up looking for Lindsey."

Woolston sat down and nodded, as if he'd heard it all before. "What about the car, Derek? You take it for a ride?"

Derek shrugged.

The detective's cell phone rang again. He listened, disconnected, then inclined his head toward Derek. "You sure there's nothing else you want to tell me?"

Derek shook his head. His foot was still tapping.

"Like how did your prints end up on the steering wheel and the trunk of the Mercedes?"

Derek flinched. That's what he'd forgotten to do at Brady's house. It was all over.

Woolston ignored him. "Where's the knife, son?"

"I didn't kill him."

"Did you have help?"

"I didn't do it. I was set up."

"It's your word against Brady's." He dropped his chin, but kept his eyes on Derek.

"I found the keys in the bar."

"So you *did* steal the car?"

Derek said nothing. It was quiet except for his shoe tapping.

"Son, if you confess, it'll go easier on you. I'll tell the States Attorney you cooperated."

"I didn't kill anyone. You can't prove it."

Woolston stood up. "You may be right. But I can put you away for theft of a motor vehicle. And with a dead body in the trunk, I can also charge you with concealing a homicide. That's a Class Three felony. With your priors, son, you're looking at some serious time."

The ceiling of the cell was dimpled with tiny white pebbles that seemed to be glued onto the tiles. Derek tried counting them as he lay on his bunk but then gave up. Some of them were so tiny he wasn't sure whether they were part of the design or just mistakes. They'd transferred him downtown after the arraignment and assigned him a public defender, but his lawyer, a woman who looked too young to know what she was doing, wanted him to cop a plea. She told him it was only a matter of time until they charged him with homicide. The only reason they hadn't was the absence of a weapon. When he told her he didn't do Lindsey, she shook her head and said it didn't much matter.

He wondered whether to tell her about the knife. It wouldn't have his prints on it, but the fact that he knew where it was might work against him. He should try to be smart about this. But he wasn't feeling very smart. Or hopeful. He should never have taken the job at Lindsey's. He'd always wanted to be a lifeguard. He should have tried for that. His parents were right. He was stupid.

He was still lying on his bed thinking how you couldn't tell day from night inside when they came to get him. Woolston was waiting for him in the interview room.

"We're letting you go," the detective said wearily.

Derek whipped his head up. "Did Brady confess?"

"No."

"Someone else did it?"

Woolston shook his head.

Derek was confused. "What happened, then?"

Woolston stared at Derek, then shrugged his shoulders. "I shouldn't be telling you this—but Brady's wife found a bloody shirt of Brady's stuffed in a bag in his closet."

Derek's chin jutted forward. "A bloody shirt?"

"Yeah. It seems that Brady and Lindsey were lovers. The wife's known about it for a while. When Lindsey showed up dead, she claims she wrestled with her conscience, hoping they could put their marriage back on track. You know, forget about the past. But when she found the shirt, she realized she couldn't."

Derek thought about it for a minute. "What does Brady say?"

"He admits that he and Lindsey were lovers. And that they had a fight the other night. But he says they made up a few minutes later. In Lindsey's office." Woolston cleared his throat.

So, that was the silence Derek heard the night he saw Brady coming out of Lindsey's office. Embarrassed, he made circles on the floor with his foot.

"Of course, Brady denies killing Lindsey, but we've got this shirt…" Woolston's voice trailed off. "And now his wife doesn't want to press charges about the car." Derek got the feeling Woolston didn't believe a thing he'd just said but didn't care enough to go on with the case. "So we're letting you go. You got lucky."

Derek smiled.

"Do me a favor, though. Get out of Chicago. It's not your kind of town."

Derek took Woolston's advice and packed his things. He'd catch a bus south. Or west. But he had one thing to do before he left. He wanted to thank Mrs. Brady for not pressing charges. Apologize for the trouble he'd caused. Tell her he hoped there were no hard feelings.

She answered the door in a halter-top and skimpy shorts. Her blond hair was swept up on top of her head.

"I've been wondering when you'd show up."

She stood close enough that he could smell her perfume. Then she turned to a small table and picked up an envelope. "I'll bet you're interested in this." She smiled mysteriously and dangled it in front of him.

"What's that?"

"You know."

"No, ma'am, I don't." He was bewildered

"Don't play dumb with me. Where is it?"

"Where's what, ma'am?" He'd been hoping to impress her with his good manners, but she didn't seem to be noticing.

"Look Derek, or whatever your name is, you almost screwed this up for me. Big time. But I managed to make it work anyway."

He shifted his feet.

"Why do you think I dropped the theft charges?"

At last, she was saying something he understood. He replied eagerly. "That's why I'm here, Mrs. Brady. I wanted to—"

She cut him off. "You're damn right that's why you're here." Derek felt like he was in one of those movies where he couldn't follow the plot. "I did you a favor. Now it's your turn. Where's the knife?"

"The knife?" Derek involuntarily took a step backwards. How could she know about the missing knife? Unless—he concentrated hard—unless she knew who put it there. Which would mean she knew who killed Lindsey. Or maybe—he met her eyes and saw the answer to his question. "You killed Lindsey."

"A real genius aren't you?" She sneered, checking her nails as if she'd just had a manicure.

"Why?"

"You think I'm just gonna sit by while my husband makes a fool of me? With another man?"

Derek thought fast now. "The keys. Brady didn't lose them. You planted them. To frame him."

She flashed him a cold smile. "After he went to sleep the other night, I took the car to the restaurant and killed Lindsey."

Derek frowned.

"Oh, I had some help." She twisted around. Derek could just make out the shape of a shirtless man sprawled on a couch in the living room. "Then we planted the keys, sopped up the shirt with Lindsey's blood and threw it in the bag with the knife. I knew Brady'd be back at Lindsey's the next morning. He was so crazy about that man he called him first thing every morning. God forbid Lindsey wasn't there, he'd run over like a damn puppy dog to find him."

"But then—"

"But then you stole the car. You really had me going for a while." She tossed her head. "I had to improvise."

Derek stuck his hands in his pockets.

"Thank God it all turned out. Now, there's only one loose end left."

She opened the envelope and peeled off a few

bills. "Consider this a down payment." She handed them to Derek. "You bring back the knife, the rest of it is yours, too."

He took the cash. Ten grand. And ten more later. He held the bills in the palm of his hand. She waited, an expectant smile on her face, while he thought it through. He stared at the floor, tiled in black and white. Then he lifted his eyes. She folded her arms across her chest. "Well?"

He chose his words with care. "You know something, Mrs. Brady? I'm right sorry, but the truth is, I just don't remember where it is. It could be anywhere." He smiled innocently.

Her smile faded.

"And if anything happens to me, the police might find a note telling them where the knife is and who used it…" his voice trailed off. He flipped up his hands.

She eyed him with suspicion, her hands on her hips. Derek bit his tongue. Finally, she sighed and handed over the rest of the cash. "You leave me no choice." Derek slid the bills into his pocket. "How do I know you'll be back?" she asked uncertainly.

"Oh, I wouldn't worry about that, ma'am," he said slyly. "I reckon you'll be seeing a lot more of me from now on."

She slammed the door in his face, but Derek

didn't mind. He whistled as he skipped down the street. He patted the twenty grand in his pocket. So what if he was dumber than dirt? Who cared if he wasn't the sharpest knife in the dishwasher? His parents were right. He had more luck than brains.

TAKING CARE OF EACH OTHER IN OUR OWN WAY

KARI KILGORE

If you're the kind to buy the bullshit the expensive glossy brochures stacked on all the business counters in town are selling, you might think Colley County, Virginia, is in the middle of some great and wonderful tourist-driven boom.

And I guess in a way, you'd be right.

We got big rowdy crowds of visitors most times of the year, hiking all over this corner of the Appalachian Mountains, demanding their favorite fancy craft beer in the highfalutin' restaurants sprouting on every street corner like mushrooms on a dead log.

Riding those blasted noisy four-wheelers and ATVs through what used to be secret valleys and pure creeks, churning every bit they can reach into sloppy mud stinking of exhaust.

Clogging up our narrow, twisty roads with their gigantic SUVs, blowing obscene amounts of money Christmas shopping for piles of "handcrafted" junk, then complaining about how much gas costs way out here in the unspoiled paradise they were the first to discover.

Well, I know who discovered what, and who did the spoiling.

But I mostly keep my head down and my mouth shut when I'm dealing with folks too ignorant to know the difference between proper home-brewed hooch and the overpriced crap they sell down at the ABC store. Even if the bottles are decorated with holly and candy canes and oh-so-sweet little snowflake scenes this time of year.

Let them have their fantasies about being the first to set foot in these pristine mountains. Especially if they keep dropping piles of that sweet tourist money everywhere they go like Hansel and Gretel's breadcrumbs.

The ones of us who live neck-deep in the kind of darkness that still lurks back in these woods—even during December's enforced-holiday-cheer bullshit—will sure take what the tourists leave behind.

And keep our own counsel when it comes to what *can* change, and what lodges itself so deep in the roots of this place that all that money, noise, and busyness they haul in never stands a chance of touching it.

Truth is, most days I wish I never touched that darkness.

But I never saw another way, and I don't expect I will now.

On the other hand, I'm what you could honestly call an entrepreneur in my own right. Not that I plan to get proper business cards made up on expensive cardstock or set up a website or smartphone app full of flashy ads and special introductory offers.

Doubt I'd find someone willing to print cards declaring *Carlis Standifer, Mess Fixer at Large: No Pile of Shit Too Hot to Handle or Too Big to Disappear* embossed in black on a fine ivory background.

Guess I could get someone to throw something up on the internet for me with all the other crap that clogs that electronic cesspool more and more every year. Trouble is I may not be all that tech savvy, but even I know not to load a digital roadmap pointing the authorities in the direction of me and my only occasionally legal line of work.

The kind of clients I tend to bring in wouldn't appreciate the attention, either.

It surely might seem strange to outsiders, including all those tourists tossing their bright and shiny money in the air so it falls like snowflakes if you live in the right part of the county.

But those of us around the grubby edges take care of ourselves—and each other—in our own way.

No, I'm a hell of a lot better off using old-fashioned word-of-mouth for my marketing.

Take the job I'm wanting to talk about, for example.

Heard from a good ol' boy named Booney Mullins with a hot automobile to get rid of. Not one he liberated from the owner himself, you understand. Not this time.

Booney swears he outgrew that kind of dumbassery thirty years ago, and so far as I hear, that's the truth.

This time it was a clear-cut case of making sure his precious kids didn't get into lifelong trouble with their youthful hellraising. Seemed like sweet-as-pie and maybe too-smart-for-her-own-good Missy Mullins had an eye for machines Daddy Mullins couldn't afford, and flexible enough morals to get them however she could.

Booney figured letting little Missy keep hot-rodding around the county's half-frozen backroads in a bright red speed demon would bring too much trouble down on her pretty head for him to tolerate. He was worried she'd get to chafing at the lack of attention or punishment or something and take her prize screaming past the Christmas lights down Main Street before too much time passed.

And the reward for information about the fine vehicle's whereabouts—but only with verified information about who removed it from its rightful home—would have been too damn high for most locals struggling to get up to the bottom to resist.

A perfect gig for a guy like me.

Because there wasn't much to do besides make that sleek automobile disappear, and without any more attention than Missy and her sweet little confused head had already stirred up.

You might be thinking the quickest, easiest thing might have been to deliver the hot hotrod to the nearest junkyard and drop it right into the car crusher. I suppose in a more prosperous area, you'd be right. The kind of place where folks have enough money or credit to order parts from the dealership, or trade the old set of wheels in for a new one once that gets to costing too much.

The good-sized towns around here are full of people like that.

Thing is—once you get outside those towns and tourists and the locals who do pretty well for themselves fleecing them—too many people in Colley County don't have that kind of scratch hidden away inside a bank or a mattress. Hell, outside the bright and shiny recreational hotspots, more than you'd think are poor and desperate enough that we've still got a disturbing number of straight-pipes shooting all the wastewater from their houses and work sheds and livestock yards right into the nearest creek.

Yeah, the head busybodies and their state environmental agency buddies are working hard as they can to bring in funding (and hefty fines) to get that mess cleaned up. At least where the out-of-town types might catch a whiff and clutch their pearls about our redneck ways.

Earns both kinds of *visitors* all kinds of friends along the way, too. The kinds of friends who don't much care for strangers knocking on their doors, much less telling them how to run the hardscrabble land their families have been surviving on for generations.

That means we don't much have car crushers in our junkyards. What we've got is acres of dead cars and trucks, surely leaking all their automotive bodily fluids right into the groundwater. And every last one of those metal skeletons slowly gets picked clean of any gasket or fuse or door handle that can be reused within a couple of days of landing in its final resting place.

Even the rusty old frames get cut up and hauled away most of the time.

So I ask you what exactly would have happened if I delivered a brand-new cherry red dream machine to a junkyard with those kinds of desperate buzzards circling all hours of the day and night, even with a couple of inches of dirty snow piled up around the edges?

Exactly. I'd have gone down, along with Missy and her concerned Daddy, and probably the junkyard owner, too.

And someone who honestly didn't wish *any* of us ill for one second would've walked away with the reward money. They'd have just been doing what they had to for a chance to survive one more day.

Only to waste every last penny on cheap Christmas crap their kids wouldn't remember by New Year's Day this time of year. Or else lottery tickets, cigarettes, and whatever poison they use to get by when the bad times drag them down low enough that the idea of kinder days ahead feels like a fairy tale twisted into a living nightmare.

But I got a better place than a junkyard above the ground for a case like this. The only inheritance worth a damn anyone in my backwoods family ever passed on down the line.

My few hundred acres of rocky hills and valleys never would draw a penny of those juicy tourist dollars, or attract any of those state environmental do-gooders with badges and clipboards keeping them from understanding the reality of life back in this washed-up tail end of the Commonwealth of Virginia.

The land was worth a damn sight more over a hundred years ago, back when it was packed full of old-growth timber and chestnuts too big for half a dozen men to get their arms around. After that goldmine was sawn to the ground and hauled off to become fine and fancy woodwork hundreds of miles away from here, those still-greedy old land barons turned their devilish ways to what was *under* the ground.

Not the kind of black gold that gets pumped up and refined and used to fill the thirsty tanks of vehicles like the speed demon I need to get rid of, either. This was the kind of black gold that got hauled off along the railroads to generate electricity. Still hundreds of miles away, and the steel our fine metallurgical coal helped refine went even further. Across the oceans to power the efforts of two world wars.

But that deep, sprawling mine played out decades ago, sometime between Korea and Vietnam.

That was when my great-great-something or other scooped up the wasted acreage to hoard like a grubby miser perched on top of a towering heap of picked-over bones. Not a lot different than the rotting hulks of the cars and trucks down at the junkyard.

But the mine's still there, entrance hidden in a mess of trash pine and scrubby underbrush that keeps it out of sight even when most trees are winter-bare. And doesn't seem like anyone besides me remembers it ever existed.

All those empty tunnels and chambers left behind after the mineral wealth departed these mountains are still there too.

You'd be surprised how many unwanted things can disappear into a cold, dark hole in the ground when the price is right. Makes a mighty fine place for what I can't get rid of in the usual ways.

That flashy, flame-colored beast wouldn't even have been the first vehicle.

But usually the things folks pay me to never see the light of day again are a lot smaller. More along the lines of things I can throw in a backpack or on the back of my own smelly pest of an ATV and haul out there.

I've never put a person down there—dead or alive—and I don't plan to. But I won't say never, and not only because I'm about to explain how I came damn close to it.

Making me borrow a beat-up tow truck from

a buddy who's more than willing to look the other way jacked up my fee considerably.

Not that my fees are ever particularly low to start with.

I guess I do my share of fleecing.

A whole bunch of people would say what I do is worse because I extract the hard-earned from my neighbors and kinfolk instead of the outsiders trampling our lands like they own it instead of just *discovering* it.

I say higher risk means higher price, and that's generally the end of that conversation.

That job, though, the one with the screaming speed machine?

It didn't end nearly so clean and easy as conversations can.

I'm not sure it ever will, at least when I try to close my eyes at night.

My serious trouble took root when I showed up at Booney Mullins' place to pick up that triple-damned car.

He's got a nice enough homestead, set back in a stand of big hardwood trees planted not long after the timber thieves stripped all the land bare and disappeared. Gravel driveway and little yard kept neat, wood-sided house painted a cheery shade of blue.

Like I said, he seems to have gotten himself straightened up, even if it didn't seem like he managed to pass his socially acceptable way of keeping his head down and his nose clean on to Missy.

Most of that hid behind two-in-the-morning darkness by the time I got there.

Backwoods part of a backwoods county or not, I wasn't about to haul an unwillingly loaned LOOK-AT-ME car away when the frigid winter sun still peeked above the ridgeline. Not even with Booney's promised tarp snugged down tight over the whole works.

I didn't see him until the belching junker of a tow truck I'd borrowed set off the glaring security light over the garage that matched his tidy little house. I knew he normally kept a few strings of Christmas lights in all his windows, but I was thankful they were all dark for business like this.

Booney never was a big man, but he seemed to have shrunk and aged in the couple of days since he asked me about the job.

He squatted by the closed garage door, staring at his boots, eyes shadowed by a baseball cap with a sharp-curved bill. Breath snaking up into the air the only sign he was alive at all.

His clothes were dark enough that I might

have missed him altogether if his face wasn't so stark and pale.

Booney waved without looking up, and he didn't move again until I climbed out of the truck and crunched across the frozen gravel toward him.

The razor-sharp night was silent except for the irritating buzz of that light, without so much as a windchill breeze. The only sounds made by a human were my footsteps.

I caught a drift of wood smoke underneath the ill-tempered truck's oily commentary. No wonder Booney or someone nearby had some kind of fire going with the cost of oil or natural gas or electricity eating their wallets alive.

Booney normally kept a reasonable dose of sense for someone who lived a fragile hair above the desperation line most days. But when he lifted his head and I finally got a good look at his hollowed-out eyes, I wasn't so sure where he'd landed.

His voice sounded nearly as rough as my boots on the gravel.

"Carlis. Appreciate you coming all the way out here, especially on a rotten night like this."

I stopped a few feet away, wondering if I shouldn't have brought someone with me. Maybe the guy who'd loaned me the truck, even if that would have cut deep into my pay and into Booney's privacy.

Still can't say what put my back up, but I learned never to ignore that particular warning long before the state finally agreed I was old enough to drive.

"Booney. Won't tell you I'm happy to do it, since I can see this is rough on you. Listen, you already told me you made up your mind, but I got to offer one more time. You sure you won't let me have someone haul that car over to the ones looking for it? They said they had to have proof of who ran off with it, but don't you think they'd be happy enough to have a toy that expensive back to shut up and walk away?"

Booney slowly got to his feet, bracing himself against the garage wall. Now, I could see how puffy his eyes were to go with the dusky signs of a ghost that had moved in to stay.

"You know I don't give a good god-damn about a reward or anything like that. Not now, and not *ever* when it comes to my kids. That's why I said no to taking it back in the first place. Too big a chance of word getting back about Missy driving it and all."

He yanked the cap off, leaving his bushy hair a spiky, dirty mess. Even back in his wild days, I never knew Booney to not keep himself up. In my experience in matters that skirt way too close to the wrong side of the law and everything else, that's never a sign of someone's mind running in the green.

Still, his face was worse.

Because when I made the mistake of looking into his eyes, whatever was tormenting him reached out and took hold of me.

His words twisted the shadow in deeper.

"Thing is, I'm not near as worried about that blasted car as I was even yesterday," he said. "I'm afraid my Missy has got herself mixed up in something worse than even jail time for theft, Carlis. Worse enough that I can't think what to do for her to get her clear."

Now, my guts twisted along with that greasy sense of something wrong.

I do a lot for the folks who hire me, or else they wouldn't give me enough of a payday to make it worth my time. If they didn't have trouble that needed my kind of help, they'd pay someone else less or fix it their damn selves.

So naturally most of the gigs that keep my bills paid and let me put a good pile back for the future aren't what most folks would call low-risk to begin with.

But as much as I can manage, I draw the line at getting mixed up in the kind of mess that could put me away for the long haul, or worse.

"You know I like to keep out of people's business as best I can," I said. "But is this something I need to know about before I get started?"

Booney crushed his hat with one hand and scrubbed his hair with the other, leaving stiff tracks and whorls behind.

"Hell, Carlis, I'm not even sure you *should* get started anymore. I wouldn't bet a tin nickel on whether to say Missy even stole that damn car or not. Never saw or heard tell of such a mess in all my life."

I made sure to keep my face as even and calm as possible, but inside my mind, I was rolling my eyes hard enough to pop them loose from their sockets. I brushed away the sweat seeping across my forehead despite the cold as I strolled toward the garage door and the set of high windows.

Pulling out a cell phone and thumbing the light on will never be as satisfying as hefting the black steel barrel of a Maglite, but a phone is a hell of a lot more handy to keep around. In any case, the phone's weak beam showed what I needed to see.

Booney had thrown the tarp over the roof of

the sleek car, as promised, but enough of the curved, muscular hood peeked through to answer one of my questions.

Another I could answer for myself.

Yeah, the car was there. And no way he or Missy came by it honestly in this lifetime.

So no way was I going through with this gig on our original terms.

"Okay then," I said. "I see the problem you called me about parked there in your garage, no arguing about that. You'll forgive me for saying so, but I doubt your girl got it saving up from odd jobs after school. What you got to decide is if you want me involved at all, Booney. But even then, I got an off-color feel about the whole job now, so I'm afraid I'll have to know more than I usually do so I can decide for myself."

He jammed the hat back on and rubbed his hands on his thighs before he started wringing his fingers together like a restless knot of earthworms he'd caught for fishing.

His words had that same kind of nervous twitchy movement.

"I wasn't lying to you the other day, or trying to trick you into something. I told you the best I knew right then. Missy wouldn't say a word about any of it until she figured out the car would be gone tonight." He held up both of his reddened hands. "I didn't say a thing to her, not once. I figure she saw where I'd put the tarp over it and worked the rest out for herself."

I shook my head.

"Doesn't matter what she knew about me or when. That's not what I was asking about."

His hands dropped and his fingers jumped right back into motion.

"No, I guess I knew that. She has the car, sure, you saw it for yourself. The trouble is *why*, and where she got it. She might even have good reason for everything, I don't know. What she said is…I don't know how much to say or how to say it without making the whole thing worse. It seems like—"

"It's okay, Daddy."

I won't try and pretend I wasn't startled, not when a teenage kid managed to sneak up on me like that. Missy had spoken from only about five feet away, in the darkness between the house and the garage.

The way she looked when she stepped out into the security light's harsh white circle downright scared me.

I'd hardly ever seen her except in passing. One of the anonymous swarm of kids that exists around the edges of your life in a small town when you don't have your own to give you an anchor point to get to know them better.

But the girl in front of us now wouldn't blend in much of anywhere.

She still had the more-or-less typical mid-teen-years local look, at least to my eyes.

Average build, pretty-but-not-beautiful face, waves of brown hair that hit right at her shoulders. The biggest difference from when I was her age more than three decades ago was I doubt she or any of the other girls had ever fried their hair (and their sense of smell) with a never-ending series of cheap perms.

Her clothes suited the weather more than Booney's did at least, but I was damn sure she'd picked out the dark scarf, hat, and gloves to make sure I wouldn't spot her before she was ready.

Something about Missy's face that night might have convinced a stranger she was a lot closer to forty—or even fifty—than almost seventeen. Her pale skin was smooth, but the dark eyes staring out at me had a strained, unnerved look.

Like she'd seen or done way too much for her years, and she might not catch up to her experiences no matter how old she got.

"Honey, this part's for me to handle."

Booney's voice was gentle as he stepped toward her. "Go on back inside, now, and let me take care of it."

Missy shook her head without looking away from me.

"No, Daddy, not this time. You always say doing adult things means I got to think about adult consequences. I guess I knew what I was getting into, so I need to face up no matter what happens."

Booney reached toward her and opened his mouth, but I held up one hand.

"How hard are you willing to work to hide things from her, Booney? Sounds to me like she'll dig until she figures it all out. Seems she can tell me what I need to know as well as you could."

Missy patted Booney's shoulder like *he* was the kid and she was the worried parent, and somehow that made me more determined to hear what she had to say. If nothing else so I wouldn't have to try to sort out two different tellings to figure out the truth.

"I can tell you a lot better since I'm the one in the middle of it." Missy crossed her arms and turned back to me, her words a lot faster, and a good deal sharper. "Daddy doesn't know most of it, but I guess he *has* to hear now that he's got you involved. Carlis Standifur, right? Someone already said I might want to get in touch with you, but Daddy did before I had the chance. Not that I could pay what you *usually* ask."

She surprised me more than desperate, angry, full-grown men usually do, and I'm ashamed to admit I blinked and twitched away from her. Worse, I had to nearly bite my tongue clean in half to keep from answering with the prompt *yes ma'am* I'd learned the hard way from two switch-wielding grannies.

The only thing that made me feel a bit less like a kindergartener with the teacher's finger pointing in my face was how Booney drew back wide-eyed himself.

I wasn't certain of much of a damn thing right then, but I knew Missy wasn't the same ordinary high school girl excited for her Christmas break she'd been not that long ago.

"You got my name right, Missy, and Booney here did ask for my help. But I'm not about to do one thing but head right back out of here until I understand what this is all about."

She shrugged. "From what I hear, you're not the kind to go dragging me off to the police. Not when you earn your wage keeping people a half-step ahead of them whether they deserve it or not.

So I might as well tell you. The car's not mine, and it wasn't exactly given to me. All I'm after is keeping one evil bastard from doing a lot worse than he already has done."

"Keep talking," I said. "You earned that much."

Her laugh ground out like shattered glass.

"Sorry if I don't say thank you for that. I'm sure you know where Triplett Holler is, over near the Kentucky line."

I only nodded. As rough as the situations I got into could be, I avoided that part of the county if I possibly could. Poverty and desperate times piled up so thick out there that people curdled and rotted, and had for decades. I have to admit the thought of Missy Mullins or any kid her age—especially a girl—out that way for any reason chilled me worse than the night air.

"You might say they've been digging for a new rock bottom when it comes to pure evil," Missy went on. "I guess dealing Oxy or running guns and cigarettes got to be too tame, or maybe too many got into it and cut the profits. Anyway, the new game they're trying to get into is running *people*."

My guts clenched, and I was glad my dinner was several hours ago.

Some might accuse me of not having any morals when it comes to who I help, but they don't know a thing about me. The lines I refuse to cross aren't the same as most folks, sure, and sometimes my lines get flexible.

But that only made the hard and sharp ones that much brighter in my mind.

"Missy, no one does that kind of thing here," Booney said, still wringing his hands. "I told you, that's all out in the big cities."

Missy seemed to swell as she rounded on him, and Booney cowered back from her.

"You're wrong about that, Booney," I cut in. "Just because we haven't had it yet doesn't mean it can't happen. Remember when we said the same thing about running drugs, before meth and Oxy took over?"

"And you still never answered my question, Daddy. About why I'd ever make something like this up. *Why?* Just let me finish and we'll see what Carlis has to say. I'm telling you Deke Triplett is doing everything he can to get in with a bunch of assholes who see women and girls as money. Men and boys too, I'm sure. He's got to prove himself before they'll let him offer up the real prize. One of his own sisters, or even daughters once he gets the chance. Then whoever he can get his nasty hands on."

I swallowed against the dread trying to claw its way up my throat.

"Tell me about the car."

Missy waved one hand toward the garage.

"*That's* the latest test he has to pass. Whoever he's trying to impress said they wanted a pretty red sleigh of their own for Christmas. Said they won't open the door to any new *elves* any other time of the year. Once he handed that over, they said, they'd see how he did bagging the reindeer." Her fierce expression cracked, and she looked from me to Booney.

"I'm sorry to say something so awful, Daddy. But that's how they put it."

"Listen, I'm not gonna pretend that couldn't happen here," I said. "I know too much about the rotten shit that goes on to say it couldn't. What I can't get a handle on is how you know any of this, Missy. I have a hard time believing you run with the kind of crowd the likes of Deke Triplett shares secrets with."

Now I could hear Booney's hands rasping together, and his breath was almost as loud.

And Missy's tough, too-adult exterior broke altogether, leaving me faced with a terrified kid who knew just how far she was in over her head. Her chin trembled, and her eyes reflected too bright under the glare.

Her voice had lost that whipcrack edge when she finally spoke.

"Because I caught Gayle Triplett crying in the locker room a week ago. We haven't much crossed paths for a long time, not since grade school after they started separating us into different classes. You know, putting the ones they think are smart together, away from the rest. Away from the poor ones too."

She stopped, breathing hard a couple of times before she could go on.

"Before that, the other kids were mean to kids like Gayle. Her clothes weren't nice, and sometimes you could tell she wasn't clean. But I got along with her back then. Maybe because I wasn't supposed to. Hardly anyone else talked to her, and that made me mad. Once we got to middle school, I guess I...I never was mean, at least I don't think so. But I wasn't as nice. Gayle learned how to keep clean, but she kind of disappeared into herself. Probably so no one would notice her."

She brushed at her cheeks with one gloved hand.

"That day in the locker room, I finally paid

attention. I sat beside her and asked what was wrong. She didn't want to tell me at first, and I don't blame her. She didn't have any reason to trust me after I basically ignored her for *years*. But I wouldn't leave, even after the bell rang. She promised to tell me after school got out, and I thought she'd never say another word to me. But she was waiting in the parking lot and told me everything."

I didn't feel the cold outside anymore over the biting freeze coming up inside, and I'm guessing Booney didn't either.

"Is Deke Gayle's father?" I said.

Missy nodded. "No one at home notices her either, so she hears *everything*. She told me about the car, how he went all the way to Louisville to grab it. How if he doesn't hand it over this week, the whole deal is off. She's scared to death that if he gets that done, he'll sell her first. Send her to a big city or out of the country. She thinks she'd be too old, except she wouldn't know enough to get away because of where she's from and how she grew up. I didn't want to tell her people like that..."

She swallowed and shook her head. Her voice shook when she went on.

"People like that know how to make just

about anyone too scared to talk. They do it all the time, or they just drug the women so they can't fight back and they *can't* get away."

Booney walked over and hugged her hard then.

The too-old version of Missy shattered, and the teenager fell apart at the same time.

She was a scared little girl, crying and holding tight to her Daddy.

"You shouldn't *ever* have to know about a thing like that," Booney said into her winter hat. "Not so long as I'm living. Why didn't you tell me, honey?"

"I don't know, Daddy," she said between wrenching sobs. "Once me and Gayle got the car away from there, I think I panicked. I was half hoping it would skid out on ice and go over the side of the mountain, or at least crash enough so no one would want it. And when you started trying to convince me we should just turn it in, I got worried they'd come after you, because *Deke* was the one offering *their* reward. And then they'd sell me right along with Gayle and I'd *never* get away."

The growl in Booney's voice was warning enough to me that the whole situation was about to get out of hand.

"They'd have to put me in the ground to get to you. But they can't do that if I put Deke Triplett down first."

Not that I thought he was wrong, not by a long shot. If Deke had been right there in front of me, I would have taken him out myself barehanded. I would have whistled while I buried his carcass in my dead coal mine, too, and made damn sure no one ever found a trace.

But knowing scum like whoever was trying to recruit his dumb ass had made it down into our mountains at all put any thought of *doing a job* right out of my mind.

"That's not what either of us are going to do, Booney, much as I agree with wanting to. We got a good chance of cutting this poison off before it digs itself in any deeper, and that's a chance we got to take."

Missy moved out of Booncy's hug, but not away from his arm around her shoulder.

"You think we can call the police? I didn't think they'd listen to a kid like me."

I surprised myself by smiling, and my cold cheeks felt like they might crack with the motion.

"Not the local cops, or even the state troopers. I'm afraid they'd get too het up and tip the wrong people off and ruin the whole thing. I never imagined I'd think of doing something like this, but we're going to the feds. This is one case where I expect you can pay for my services just fine, Missy. All I ask is something hot to drink."

She smiled in return, and I finally got a glimpse of the typical sixteen-year-old Booney had been so worried about.

And misunderstood so badly.

"Then both of you get inside and out of this cold," she said. "I'll build up the fire and Daddy can make some of his amazing hot chocolate, and I'd bet we can find something good to go with it."

At least for now, the brittle, painful adult shell of everything she'd learned way too young gave way and let Missy shine through.

I'll tell you something else I never would have believed.

Right then, seeing her that way was reward enough for me.

The season got behind us and into spring before I had a chance to speak to Booney and Missy without some variety of law enforcement around us like vultures, looking to snatch up any crumb of information they could get.

I guess that sounds uncharitable of me to say after they managed to bust open a nasty piece of work like a human trafficking ring that was about ready to ramp up operations, and I can't argue with that.

All I can say is the habits of a long hardscrabble lifetime die hard, kind of like my old line of work.

Sure, I pay my bills more or less the same way I always did, even if I laid pretty low while snow was on the ground that year. I figure I'll do the same once the weather heats up and the cops cool down.

It was Missy herself who invited me back over to their place one afternoon.

Easter Sunday as a matter of fact. My own mother and grannies and a whole swarm of aunties might not like a bunch of things about my general observations of their churchgoing ways. So me getting myself scrubbed up enough for company and wearing a nice shirt and even a tie would have made them proud.

Booney and Missy and probably her older brother and sisters had tidied up the yard a good bit to go with the late break in the weather. Cleared away winter's dead branches and flattened grass, planted a bunch of daffodils and such to brighten up the yard. I suspected the garage had a new coat of paint, but I wasn't ready to swear to that.

The air smelled like growing things instead of stinking like paint. Still, you never know with the new stuff they make these days for folks that can afford it.

Word was Booney had come into some kind of reward money after all, but not from the pure monsters who were after the since-returned red hotrod that started the whole mess.

I figured that was none of my business unless he wanted to tell me, and that made it none of anyone else's business why his place seemed so much happier now.

Seeing Missy's smile light up the already sunny day when she opened the door might have given me that impression. That and the shy, hesitant smile of the girl who stepped out behind her.

Someone who didn't know any better might not notice Gayle Triplett standing there, in her dark blue church dress compared to Missy's fluffy Easter pink. Gayle's auburn hair hung in a braid down her back that kind of disappeared beside Missy's cheery brown curls.

But I knew how much Gayle's little smile meant, and I was damn glad to see it.

"Hey Carlis," Missy said. "Thank you for coming by! I hope you brought an empty belly with you, because we've been getting ready for Easter Brunch all weekend long. Got everything almost ready at the picnic table out back."

"I guess I could put a bunch of good home cooking away. Glad to see both of you looking happy."

Missy turned toward Gayle, waiting like I was for her to get a chance to say something after not being noticed for too damn long.

"It's a happy day, Mr. Standifur," Gayle said, stronger than I expected, even with her cheeks turning red. "I'm glad to get to say thank you. For everything."

"You're welcome, Gayle. Much appreciated. Hope you'll decide to call me Carlis someday when you're ready."

Booney stepped outside, shined up himself in his church suit, jacket and all.

"You two want to head out back and finish? Me and Carlis will be there in a minute."

Missy rolled her eyes and giggled, and Gayle's answering grin managed to warm my own shriveled heart. They scurried off.

"Good to see you, Booney. Everything working out all right?"

He laughed and tried to brush back his silver and brown curls, but the breeze just sprung them back up again.

"As well as it can work out in a house with twice the teenage girl that I'm used to lately. Good thing me and Margaret raised more than one before she passed, God rest her. I guess we'll figure it out as we go."

"Seems like they're real good for each other."

"Yeah, Gayle leaves a little bit more of the bad parts behind her every day. I know Missy still has bad dreams sometimes, but they talk to each other all the time. Listen, I'm not sure how much you hear around town, or how much of what you do hear is bullshit. I guess you're one of the few who honestly cares about what's going on."

The rumors and gossip had flown thicker than normal once news of Deke Triplett's arrest got out, and still bubbled up more than usual. Bad as the things he got accused of were, hardly any of the tales hit twisted and sick enough as the truth.

"I assume most of it *is* bullshit, like I always did. I'm guessing the ones that disappeared not long after Deke will end up where he is."

Booney nodded. "He'd dug up a handful as devilish as he is to help him on the road to hell. Truth is we cracked that shell just in time. Well,

Gayle and Missy did. The feds followed the chain a good ways up the line, so more than Colley County is in the clear now. Got more women and girls than I want to know about away from them too."

I focused on the bobbing yellow mass of daffodils instead of letting my mind run off in that direction. It had done enough of that when I tried to sleep back in the winter.

"I guess sometimes we get a chance to balance the scales a little," I said. "Put some good back where we never bothered to before."

"That's just exactly how I feel about taking Gayle in. I may not be able to help the other ones, but I can do my best by her. Might even adopt her if the state says I can. And if she wants me to."

He reached out and gripped my shoulder.

"This business started off in a real bad way, Carlis, but I'm glad you were here. Whether we meant to or not, we did a whole lot of good. I thank you for that."

I smiled and patted his shoulder back. I'm used to people saying rotten things to me, or nothing at all.

Learning how to handle folks saying something nice is gonna take a lot more practice.

"Much appreciated, and right back at you,

Booney. I reckon we better get back there before those girls decide to come after us."

As we laughed and started that way, I knew sometimes it was worth digging out the good things from the bad, no matter how hard times get all around us.

And grabbing our chances to take care of each other in our own way might be the best thing of all.

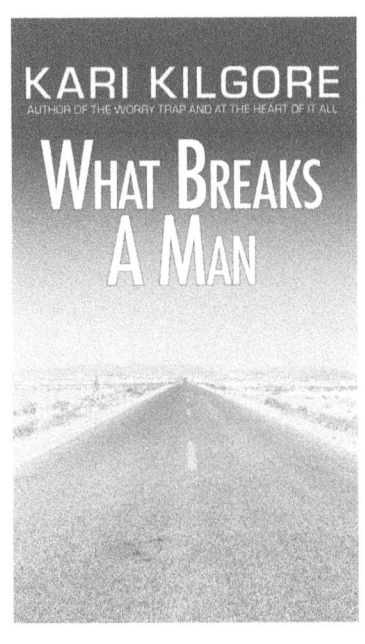

MYSTERIOUS TALES FROM KARI KILGORE

PAST, PRESENT, FUTURE
ACROSS MOUNTAINS, CITIES, AND
INTO THE IMAGINATION

JOIN THE ADVENTURE
www.KariKilgore.com/Mystery

Kari's short story "What Breaks a Man" was listed in Best American Mystery and Suspense's Other Distinguished Mystery and Suspense of 2021

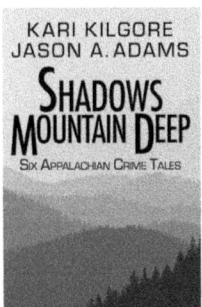

PAY UP OR WALK TO SCHOOL

CHRIS CHAN

I'm not a big sports guy, but when the Cuthbertson Hall boys' varsity basketball team won a game against their arch-rivals, Bluemound Academy, with a last-second three-point shot, winning by a single point, I couldn't help but be caught up in general uproar of triumph. The moment passed, and while most of the students were doing a frenzied dance on the court, I nudged my girlfriend Nerissa, and suggested that we head out before the mad rush to leave caused a traffic jam in the parking lot.

She agreed, and we said a few quick goodbyes to the other teachers before slipping out the side door. I was in the process of turning left towards my car when I heard an anguished howl, and the two of us wrapped our long coats around us to block the wind as we turned around and hurried towards a corner of the parking lot, where three Cuthbertson students were standing around a cardboard sign placed in the middle of a space.

I recognized them at once. For the purposes of this account, I will refer to them as Arlo, Odell, and Ranger. All of them were seniors on the hockey team. The reasons why I cannot use their real names will become obvious over the course of this narrative. The three boy were notorious troublemakers, but they certainly weren't malicious kids, just mischievous. As we approached them, Arlo was kneeling on the ground in front of the sign, screaming at the sky with his fists in the air. Odell and Ranger were standing behind him, comforting him.

Arlo turned towards us. "Someone stole my car!" His eyes crinkled, as if he was trying to cry and failing.

"What is he going to do?" Odell asked.

"This is terrible, just terrible." Ranger made his own unsuccessful attempt at crying.

I knew that the three of them were up to something. There was a reason why they were all on the hockey team and not the stars of the drama club. Whatever was happening, I realized that they weren't behaving naturally.

Nerissa and I took a moment to read the sign. The square of white cardboard was about two feet square, and appeared to be cut from the side of a box. It was stuck in one of the orange traffic cones that were used to cordon off a corner of the parking lot that had potholes being repaired. A couple of notches had been cut into the top of the cone, allowing it to serve as a stand for the sign. The words on the sign were composed of block letters and were written in black marker.

WE HAVE TAKEN YOUR CAR
THE RANSOM IS $100
PAY UP OR WALK TO SCHOOL
WAIT FOR INSTRUCTIONS

I noticed a black Sharpie sticking out of Odell's jacket pocket, but I chose not to say anything. Nerissa gave me a little nudge and a nod in the direction of his pocket, and I returned the nod to inform her I'd seen it too.

"Who could have done this? Who?" Arlo asked.

"And why would that person only ask for $100?" I wondered. "After all, the profit margin isn't very high considering the risk."

None of the three boys seemed to have any reply to that. "Perhaps this isn't a very smart criminal," Odell ventured.

"I was just thinking that," I replied. "Shall I call the police?"

"No!" All three boys shouted at the top of their lungs, and Nerissa and I shared a glance, confirming our mutual suspicion that something was not quite right with this supposed stolen car scenario.

"I don't want to risk them keeping my car," Arlo explained. "$100 is worth it to me."

"How are you going to get home?" Nerissa asked.

"Oh, my car's here," Odell explained. "I'll take him to his house."

"I think you should let me know when you hear from the people who stole your car," I told them.

"I will," Arlo promised.

The three of them started to hurry away, and Nerissa called out to them, "Shall we take the sign? Who knows? There might be fingerprints on it."

"There aren't—I don't think there'll be fingerprints on it," Odell answered, twisting his hands, which were encased in black leather gloves. "The people who did this, they're probably professionals."

"Professionals who only ask for a hundred bucks?" The three boys didn't seem interested in my question, choosing instead to jog away without so much as a "good night."

By that point, the parking lot was filled with people heading home, and we figured that if we tried to leave now, we'd be stuck waiting in line for twenty minutes, so we might as well pick up the sign and store it in my office. A closer look revealed that there were indeed partial fingerprints on the back of the sign—tiny ridges left in black marker ink. It's challenging to use a black permanent marker for any length of time without smearing your fingers and spreading the mess on the writing surface.

"How much do you want to bet that these prints will match those of one of the three boys?" I asked Nerissa.

"That's a sucker's bet," she replied. "The real question is which one of them wrote this. I'd say it was Odell. I've had all three of them in at least one of my classes over the years, and of the three, Odell's the most careful and thoughtful. The penmanship here is pretty good—the letters are nice and even. I bet he wrote the sign. Plus the marker in his jacket pocket."

"So if this is all some sort of scam, what do they hope to gain by it? Is it some sort of insurance fraud?"

Nerissa shrugged and brushed a stray thread off of her brown suede trench coat. "I have a feeling we'll find out more tomorrow."

She was completely right. The next day, before the start of classes, the three boys showed up at my office. Arlo was holding a letter made with letters that had been cut and pasted from a magazine. "I found this pushed through my mail slot today," he informed me.

Though I didn't state this fact aloud, I knew that professional criminals almost never cut and paste letters and words from magazines and newspapers. It's a Hollywood trope that rarely appears in reality. The note read:

PUT THE MONEY THE CAN AND THROW IT IN THE CREEK BY THE SCHOOL

"What can?" I asked.

"This one." Arlo pulled a coffee can out of his backpack. "I found it outside the house, in front of the mail slot."

"Huh," I said as I examined the note.

"What?" Odell wiped a droplet of sweat from his brow as he asked the question. I noticed that there were little black marker smears on the side of his hand.

"There's no creasing or bowing on the letter. You'd think whoever wrote this would have had to fold it or roll it up to fit it through the mail slot."

After an awkward pause, Arlo replied, "We have a large mail slot."

"Ah, that explains it." I don't know how successful I was at keeping a straight face.

"I'm going to pay the ransom right now." Arlo pulled an envelope out of his left jacket pocket and showed me the hundred-dollar bill inside. "Want to come with us?" he asked as he replaced the envelope in his pocket.

Deciding that it was best to watch this situation play out, I pulled on my walking coat and followed Arlo and the other two boys outside. It was a two-minute walk to the little creek that runs alongside the school's grounds. Once we reached the creek's edge, Arlo pulled an envelope out of his right jacket pocket, placed it in the coffee can, affixed the lid, and tossed the can into the water, where the current carried it away.

"I suppose the thieves will pick it up somewhere down the line," Ranger remarked.

After a noncommittal "Hmm" from me, the four of us walked back to school and the boys hurried off to their classes. Back in my office, I leaned back in my chair and thought. I knew that I was being had, but I didn't know exactly what the goal of this deception was. I had to wrap up a background check on a prospective hire in the groundskeeping department, so I decided to wait and see what happened with the whole car ransoming situation.

I didn't wait long. Half an hour before lunch, the trio reappeared at my office door. "I just got a text," Arlo informed me. "It says that my car is parked in the furniture store lot just under a mile north of here. Can I please have permission to go get it?"

A couple of seconds of consideration later, I replied, "Certainly." The boys had a free period, so they weren't missing any classes. The trio travelled in Odell's car, and I followed behind them. Maybe all three of them didn't have to come along, but I wanted to watch their faces.

Two minutes of driving, and Arlo was reunited with his car. There was no damage that I could see. I tried the driver-side door and found that it was locked. Arlo fished his keys out of his pocket, and as he opened the door, I commented, "Thoughtful of them to lock the door. And you must have a couple of bucks in change in that cupholder. They didn't touch that."

"I guess they can't be that bad."

"I wonder how they started the car? You have your keys, and there's no sign of tampering to start the car, such as fiddling with the wires or something like that."

Arlo was at a loss for words, and Odell looked nervous enough to faint. Finally, Ranger said, "They must be great at their jobs. We'd better get back so we don't miss lunch."

My growling stomach led me to agree with him, and we made it back with plenty of time to eat. When I told the story to Nerissa over tuna noodle casserole, we both agreed that something was up with the trio. We were pretty sure it wasn't a prank on us, but I was certain that they were trying to manipulate me somehow. Sometimes all you can do is wait and see what happens.

I didn't have to wait long. That evening there was a hockey game at Cuthbertson. I was busy working with the security team, making sure that the cars were secure. I'd informed the trio that I'd be watching to prevent another auto theft, and they seemed less than enthusiastic about my vigilance. After three hours of driving around the lots, staring at security cameras, and a quick conversation with a seventy-year-old grandmother of a hockey player who was trying to get into someone else's car that just happened to be the same make and model as hers, I made my way home. Nerissa had spent the evening with her family, and right after I got back I called her to let her know that there'd been no new car thefts. Moments after we said "good night," my phone rang. It was Odell, telling me in a remarkably calm voice that his car had been stolen.

Fortunately, I hadn't even taken off my coat, so once he'd given me his address, I had a four-mile drive to his house. As I pulled into the driveway, I saw Odell holding a white cardboard sign. It was very similar to the last one, saying:

**WE HAVE TAKEN YOUR CAR
THE RANSOM IS $1000
PAY UP OR WALK TO SCHOOL
WAIT FOR INSTRUCTIONS**

"The price has gone up tenfold," I noted.

"I can afford it," Odell assured me.

"Where are your parents?"

"They're in Hawaii. They're taking a vacation with Ranger's father and stepmother."

"So you're on your own?""

"Yeah. Why do you ask?"

"I just wanted to know if there were any witnesses?"

My questions seemed to have unnerved Odell, but he relaxed a bit. As he ran a hand over his forehead, I noticed a few black marker stains on his hand that weren't there earlier. "No, I don't think anybody saw anything." Odell's house was in the middle of a thickly wooded area, so none of the neighbors would have been likely to observe whatever happened.

"What happened? Were you carjacked? Were they waiting for you with a gun?"

"No, nothing like that. I didn't see them. I got home, walked into the house, and as I was hanging up my jacket, I heard the engine start. By the time I got outside, the car was gone. And this sign was leaning against the garage."

"Was there a rock on it or something like that?"

"No, why?"

"It's lucky you went outside as soon as you did. With this wind, the ransom note could've blown away. It would've been luckier if you'd managed to get a glimpse of the thieves, though."

"I didn't see them," he sounded so adamant that my suspicious instincts prickled, but I let the point go. After asking him to tell me as soon as he heard from the thieves, I headed home, with a pretty good idea of what to expect the next morning.

My guess was pretty close. I was expecting Odell to show me another ransom note with cut-and-pasted letters. As soon as I showed up at work, Odell and his pals showed me another text, telling him:

PUT $1000 IN AN ENVELOPE AND GO BEHIND THE ICE RINK

"Have you tried calling the number that sent this text?' I asked.

"I told him not to risk it," Ranger informed me. "They might freak out, and anyway, it's probably a burner phone."

I stared at him for a good five seconds before agreeing with him. "Shall we check out the ice rink?" I asked.

We made our way there and found a beautiful black Labrador Retriever tied with a leash to one of the pipes running along the side of the building. A big fanny pack was strapped around his neck. There was a little note rolled up and stuck under his collar. It was printed in black marker—what else? —and said,

PUT THE MONEY IN THE FANNY PACK AND LET THE DOG GO

As Odell pulled a sealed envelope out of his pocket, I asked him, "Are you sure that there's exactly $1,000 there? If you miscounted and there's only nine hundred-dollar bills in there, there might be trouble."

Odell froze for a moment before saying, "I checked. It's fine."

"Don't you want me to take note of the serial numbers?"

"No!" All three boys shouted so loudly that they made each other jump.

"I just want to get my car back!" Before I could respond, Odell shoved the money into the fanny pack and unclasped the leash. The dog bounded away like a rocket, sprinting northward. It was out of my sight in just over twenty seconds.

So the day continued normally, and during the midday break, Odell told me he'd gotten another text telling him his car was in the parking lot by the frozen yogurt shop down the road from school. I knew I couldn't miss this, so Ranger drove him down with me following, and we found his car in a corner of the lot. Despite not having the keys, the thieves had left the car locked and in perfect condition, and they hadn't touched the laptop that Odell had left in the back seat. After the boys headed back to school, I bought myself a cupful of chocolate brownie frozen yogurt and went back to work.

That evening, Nerissa and I caught a movie, which was a pretentious lump of Oscar bait that neither of us enjoyed. As we left the theater, I turned my phone back on to discover that Ranger had left me a message. He asked me to come to his house at once, because his father's car had been stolen. When we arrived, the trio all walked out of the garage to meet us. Ranger was holding the white cardboard sign this time. It read:

**WE HAVE TAKEN YOUR DAD'S CAR
THE RANSOM IS $100,000
PAY UP OR WALK TO SCHOOL
WAIT FOR INSTRUCTIONS**

I recognized Ranger's car in the driveway. "They took your father's car."

"Right."

"But you still have yours. Why would you have to 'walk to school?'"

None of the boys had any answer for that. "What kind of car does your father have?" Nerissa asked.

"A sapphire blue Bentley Flying Spur." That meant nothing to Nerissa, and all I knew about the car is that it was probably extremely expensive.

"Walk me through your evening," I told them.

PAY UP OR WALK TO SCHOOL

Ranger cleared his throat. "After hockey practice we went out for pizza with some other guys. When we were done hanging out, the three of us came back to my place to play some video games, and when we got here, Dad's car was missing."

"Was the garage door open? I can ask your neighbors, one of them might have seen it open or shut, which can help pin down the time of the crime."

Looking apprehensive at my question, Ranger stalled for a moment before saying, "It was closed. No one would have noticed anything."

Nerissa wandered over to the recycling bins. "What are you doing?" Odell sounded panicky.

"I saw this sticking out..." Nerissa opened the lid to reveal the remains of a white cardboard box. Three sides of it had been cut away.

"The thieves must have thrown that away here!" Ranger exclaimed.

That wasn't a bad response, but I wondered, "Why would they leave a perfectly good square of cardboard behind? Don't you think they'll strike again?"

"Maybe they're done for now?" Arlo suggested, putting a couple of seconds of pausing between each word. "What if they're not greedy and they think they've made enough money?"

"I wonder why they'd target you three and then stop. And anyway, they haven't gotten the third ransom yet, have they?" I asked. "Ranger, do you have a hundred grand free?"

"Ahh...no."

"Any chance of getting it by morning? Because if the pattern holds, you're going to get a message telling you to pay up first thing tomorrow."

"No! There's no way I could possibly get that much money. And anyway, it's my Dad's car, not mine. But he's not here." Ranger's tone was surprisingly laid-back.

"That's right, he's not." I shared another look and had a quick nonverbal conversation with Nerissa. A quick check of my watch told me it was nearly nine, and I decided that the trio had taken up enough of my night. "All right, I'm done with this."

"What do you mean, Mr. Funderburke?" Ranger was trying to look innocent, but he only succeeded in appearing smug.

"Where's the car? Or rather, what's left of it?"

Now Ranger was failing at sounding indignant. "What are you implying, Mr. Funderburke? Do you think that we had something to do with this?"

"Let me tell you a bit about what I was up to earlier today," I informed him. "I made a call to some local police stations. Turns out, three days ago, there was a report of three teenaged boys matching your description sitting on a park bench, scarfing fast food and drinking beer. A concerned citizen saw underage drinking and went to confront the boys. They ran off, leaving their beer cans and food wrappers behind, jumped into a bright blue car, and sped away. The concerned citizen told the police, and they gave me her contact information. I showed her the most recent Cuthbertson Hall yearbook, and she identified you three as the ones she'd seen."

"It was dark," Ranger stammered. "She couldn't see clearly. It wasn't us."

"How did you know it was after sunset?" Nerissa asked. "Funderburke said 'three days ago.' The incident could have taken place during daylight hours. You just proved that you were there."

None of the trio had any reply to make. I was enjoying the quiet, but I knew I had to keep talking. "Here's what I think happened. Your father and stepmother are out of town, Ranger, you're on your own and you decided to take your father's car on a joyride. You were driving around, you were drinking. Along the way, somewhere where there probably weren't any witnesses, you had an accident. Not just a dent, something huge. I don't know if the car was totaled or not, but probably it was. Whatever happened, the damage couldn't be hidden or fixed. I don't know where the car is now. The garage of someone you know? Covered up in some wooded area? Pushed into a lake or river?"

"Oh, geez." From the looks on Arlo and Odell's faces as I said that last one, I figured I'd hit the mark. After taking a moment to wonder which local body of water held the remains of the Bentley Flying Spur, I continued. "So you decided to come up with a story that it was stolen. However, you thought it might be less suspicious if you created the impression that it was part of a broader car theft ring, which was silly. If you'd broken the garage window or something, it would've been easier to believe in a simple crime. When you created this improbable ransom demand situation, I got suspicious immediately."

"I told you it was a dumb idea," Odell moaned.

"Shut up," Ranger hissed.

"Why did you only ask for $100 for the first car?" Nerissa asked.

Arlo barely managed a whisper. "It was all I had handy."

"You switched out the envelopes, of course," I added. "I noticed you used a different pocket. So you threw an empty envelope in the coffee can and tossed it in the creek. By the way, that was another amateur move to use cut-and-paste letters. No real criminal does that. Too messy and time-consuming."

"Toldja," Odell snapped at Ranger. "It did take forever. That's why we switched to the text the second time."

I nodded. "That's what I figured. You parked the car before school and made a big show when you arrived to retrieve it. I guess the next go-round, you repeated the process and upped the ransom to raise the stakes, but you didn't have a thousand dollars handy. What was it? Just cut-up paper?" Odell nodded, and Ranger howled at him to keep his mouth shut. "Where'd you get the dog?"

"He belongs to my neighbor," Odell explained. "He knows how to find his way home. My neighbors work late, so I took off the fanny pack when I came back from school. They never missed him."

"How were you planning to handle the third

ransom payment? The one you couldn't pay?" I asked.

"I was going to pilot my brother's toy drone," Arlo explained. "Ranger was going to leave a note saying he didn't have the money, I'd fly the drone away and bring it back with a note saying, 'Too bad, you'll never see the car again.' We thought that would explain the missing car."

"What are you going to do now?" Odell asked.

"He can't do anything. We haven't broken any laws," Ranger snapped.

I shrugged. "Throwing the coffee can in the creek was littering. Technically borrowing the Labrador Retriever was dognapping."

"But no one got hurt," Ranger reminded me. "We can say the stolen cars were all a prank, that it was all just fun and games."

"What about your Dad's car?" I asked. "Where is it?"

"It's in the lake in this park a couple miles north of here," Arlo blurted out over Ranger's howls of protest. "Ranger drove it into a tree and it crumpled up like a soda can. It's a miracle we weren't hurt. We weren't thinking clearly, so we pushed it forty yards into the lake."

"I need to tell the parks department."

Ranger seemed incensed by my comment. "You don't need to tell them anything. You're the Student Advocate. You're supposed to protect us."

"I'm supposed to help you when you're in trouble. I am not your fixer for problems that you created. I don't cover up your misdeeds. Besides, how are you going to handle the missing car? When your father tries to file an insurance claim, they'll put their top investigators on it, and I assure you they will find the car, and they will figure out what happened. And then it might be a criminal matter."

Arlo and Odell looked petrified. Ranger just looked angry. "So what do we do?" Arlo whispered.

We talked it over for a bit, and eventually Ranger realized that there was no escaping his father's wrath, and I saw no need to punish Arlo and Odell for their participation in a frankly ridiculous scheme, at least in a school setting. So I turned them over to their parents, and their consciences were bugging them so badly that they confessed everything, and got a week's grounding each.

Ranger's father, I was soon to learn, had anger management issues, and I had to step in to protect the kid from serious bodily harm. After a lot of shouting on the part of Ranger's father, Ranger moved out of the nice, big house and into his mother's tiny apartment. Apparently she hadn't read the pre-nup thoroughly before signing it. Ranger's father confiscated his son's car, and his college fund, and bought himself a new Bentley Flying Spur, this time in emerald green, and took much better care of it than he did his own son.

Fortunately for Ranger, he managed to get a full hockey scholarship to a university in northern New York, but he had no extra money for a new vehicle. When he started college, his dorm was over a mile from the main campus, so every morning in an icy climate, he had to walk to school.

ALWAYS GONNA HAPPEN

JOSLYN CHASE

Six months after Davy Larkins was shanked to death in the Monroe Correctional Complex for Men, he joined Sherman Tate on the outside, on the day of his release.

Sherman wasn't surprised to see him. They'd always been close, even when they weren't sharing a cell.

"Whatcha gonna do now, Sherm? You're out, free as a bird, with a whole new world of steel for the picking."

Sherman blinked. He rubbed his damp palms down the front of his denim work pants. "Oh no, Davy," he said. "No more car thugging for me. I aim to stay out this time."

Davy laughed. "Right."

Sherman locked his jaw and lifted his chin. He wanted Davy to know he was serious. Davy saw and changed his tone. "Can you do that, Sherm? You heard what the warden said when he was walking you to the gate."

"Yes, I heard it. I ain't deaf. He said stealing cars is all I know how to do and I'll be back in two shakes of a lamb's tail. But he's wrong, Davy. I can do it this time. I know I can."

"Sure, sure." Davy lifted an arm. "But what about that little beauty over there? Can you walk right by that without a second glance?"

Sherman stopped in his tracks, a low whistle rising up out of his throat. Davy was pointing to a sky blue Lancia Stratos, circa 1970, in pristine condition. A rare and beautiful beast. Salivary glands firing on overdrive, Sherman swallowed hard and clenched his fists.

"Watch me, Davy. Watch me pass it by, face forward, never looking back."

Sherman marched past. Every step felt like he was wearing cast-iron shoes, but he didn't stop until he turned the corner, and the Lancia was out of sight.

"Hot damn," Davy said. "You're really going straight."

"I really am," Sherman agreed.

And he meant it. Right up until the day the gods pulled back the clouds and dropped a fat juicy plum in his lap.

He and Davy were sharing a bag of greasy fries from a diner on the outskirts of downtown Seattle. Just walking and killing time before reporting in for work.

Sherman almost missed it, came so close to

shuffling past without noticing, but Davy spotted it and clapped him on the back.

"There she is, Sherm," he said, pointing to the black Toyota Camry parked at the curb. "All fired up and waiting for you."

Sherman saw what he meant. The car was running, smooth motor humming, key in the ignition, doors unlocked.

And no one inside.

"It's meant to be, bro," Davy said. "Don't deny it, don't fight it. Just go." He cast his gaze around, eyes a little wild, a cunning grin curving his lips. "Go like the wind, Sherm."

Davy was right. There was no fighting it, not when it was so clearly ordained.

Sherman didn't remember opening the door, sliding into the seat, or peeling away from the curb. It was like a dream, not quite coherent. Not quite real.

Until the blare of sirens snapped him back to cold, hard, in-your-face reality.

Heart ratcheting up in his chest, Sherman turned to Davy. But the passenger seat was empty. He didn't know what to do, so he just kept driving, taking the turns at random.

Four blocks later, the whine of the sirens faded into the distance and Sherman's chest loosened up enough so he could pull in a full, deep breath.

He saw a sign for the I-90 entrance ramp and merged onto the freeway, heading east. As he pulled to the inside lane and passed a moving van, Davy climbed over the seat and sprawled against the door, giving Sherman a gleeful thumbs up.

"Whew! What a rush."

Sherman said nothing.

"Hey, don't feel bad, man. It was always gonna happen. Today just turned out to be the day."

"Shut up, Davy. What am I supposed to do now?"

"Do you want me to shut up, or tell you what you're supposed to do?"

Sherman thought. "Tell me."

Davy stared out the window for a long time. At last, he said, "I don't know. Just keep driving while we figure it out."

Sherman drove. He stayed mostly in the right-hand lane, obeying the speed limit and remembering to use his turn signal when called for. Traffic was heavy until they got past Issaquah where it thinned out, allowing him to get a good look at the vehicles behind him in the rearview mirror.

A cop car was coming up fast.

Vehicles leapt out of the passing lane to let the patrol car go by, and it was gaining on the little Camry at an alarming rate. As it drew within ten car lengths, the flashers flared on and a high-pitched wail raised the hairs on the back of Sherman's neck.

"What do I do, Davy?"

Davy gripped the dashboard. "Go down with the ship, Sherm. Don't pull over."

Sherman tightened his hands on the steering wheel and pressed his foot to the floor.

The police car zipped past, shaking the Camry in its wake.

Before Sherman could even heave a sigh of relief, a *ding* sounded from the instrument panel and the fuel light came on, burning like an angry red eye.

"End of the road, dude," Davy said, "but we knew it was always gonna happen. Let's get off the freeway and find a place to ditch this ride."

Hands shaking, heart still hammering in his chest, Sherman signaled and exited, guiding the car down the off-ramp. He turned right at the first intersection and took another right two miles down the road.

He had no idea where he was going, and he didn't think Davy knew either.

Tall pines lined both sides of the winding asphalt, swaying in the stiffening breeze. Afternoon was waning into evening and lights twinkled at sparse intervals as they passed small clusters of houses or shops.

Sherman drove until the engine started to cough. He turned off on a narrow dirt lane running beside an empty field and let the car coast to a stop.

"Fun while it lasted, wasn't it, bro?" Davy said.

Adrenaline still rushing in his veins, Sherman had to agree. "But what now?" he asked.

Davy raised a finger, like a teacher calling the class to attention. "Now, we wipe the car clean and get the hell out of here. Just leave it and find a bus station somewhere."

"Okay."

Using the tail of his shirt, Sherman wiped down all the surfaces he or Davy might have touched. He pushed the driver's seat all the way back so the cops wouldn't be able to tell how tall their car thief had been.

A gust of wind ruffled his hair as he climbed out of the car, and he shivered. "It's cold. I don't want to walk all over hill and dale without a jacket."

Davy peered in the windows of the back seat.

"Check the trunk. Maybe there's something there you can wrap up in."

Sherman found the lever and popped the trunk. He lifted the lid.

Heart flopping in his chest, he stared down at the trunk's contents.

"Holy Mackerel!" Davy said. "Am I seeing what I think I'm seeing?"

Sherman reached out a hand and loosened the neck of one of the canvas drawstring bags. Bundled stacks of bills spilled out onto the floor of the trunk. A bolt of white-hot excitement shot through him.

Followed by a jolt of ice-cold fear.

"Where was this car when we found it?" he asked Davy.

Davy gripped his arm, still staring at the cash. "Somewhere on 31st Avenue, wasn't it?"

"I think it was. Right in front of—"

Davy gasped. "The bank! Dude, you grabbed the getaway car!"

Sherman's stomach twisted in his gut. "You're the one who—"

"Doesn't matter now, bro. You're deep in a crap hole. Not only are the cops after you..."

"The robbers are, too."

"Oh, yeah. They're sure to be pissed you stole

their money *and* their ride after everything they did to get it. They'll hunt you and gut you like a ten point buck."

"What do I do, Davy?"

Davy blew out a long breath. "I hate to say it, but you can't take the cash. You'd be signing your death warrant."

"Well, I'm not just leaving it here."

"No, you're right. That would be a bad idea, too."

Shivering and miserable, Sherman hugged himself and listened to the wind rustling across the field. He opened his mouth to speak, but Davy cut him off.

"If you're thinking about turning it over to the authorities," he said, "you might as well just buy a one-way ticket back to Monroe."

"You got a better idea?"

"Matter of fact, I do, Sherm. You got a lighter?"

"You're going to burn the money?"

"Hell, no! We're going to hide the money and burn the car."

Sherman looked at the black Camry, regret knifing through him. He felt a fondness for the little car.

"Why do we have to burn it, Davy? We wiped it real clean. Let's just walk away."

"We wiped it clean when we thought the cops would be looking for a small-time car thief. For a bank robber, they'll pull this car into their fancy lab and go over it with a fine-tooth comb. They'll find your DNA, Sherm, and you'll go down."

Sherman kicked the rear tire. "Guess you're right, Davy."

"Course I am. Don't just stand there—go scrounge up some dried leaves."

Glad to give his shaking hands something to do, Sherman clambered through the strip of woodland next to the field, gathering handfuls of crackling leaves. As he scooped up a pile in front of a creaking oak tree, he saw a large hollow at the base of the trunk.

Big enough to hide the sacks of bills.

He and Davy stuffed the three bags of cash into the old dry cavity and found a large stone to cover the hole. They built a mound of dirt over and around it and scattered more dead leaves to hide their handiwork.

"That ought to do for now," Davy said. "Let's finish this and get out of here."

Back at the car, they stuffed the gas tank full of leaves and tinder and pushed a lit tree branch inside, fanning the blaze until it took hold and the Camry roared into flame.

Sherman stared, mesmerized by the flames and saddened by the Camry's pitiful demise.

"Don't let this get you down," Davy said. "It was always gonna happen."

They spent the rest of the night hiking in the dark, hitching rides, and waiting around at bus stops until dawn brought Sherman to the door of his crappy motel room.

He was so tired he hadn't even noticed Davy was no longer with him. Pushing his way inside, he collapsed on the bed and grabbed the remote, pointing it toward the TV. He thumbed through the channels and found a news report with footage of a plastic-faced blonde speaking into a mic on 31st Avenue in front of the bank.

Turning up the volume, he leaned back against a stack of pillows and listened to her account.

"...armed robbers were killed in the firefight with police, except for the driver who got away with the money before responders arrived at the scene. In a bizarre twist, the man believed to be the getaway driver was hit by a bus later last night and pronounced DOA at Harborview Medical Center."

"Looks like case closed, Judy. I understand that

police believe all participants in the attempted robbery lost their lives during the crime."

"That's right, Jim. The only remaining mystery is what happened to the money."

"A mystery indeed. It appears the only one who knew took the answer to his grave."

Davy thunked down on the bed next to Sherman and gave his thigh a slap.

"Hot damn, Sherm! Looks like you're off scott-free. No one even knows you were there. Told you it was meant to be."

Sherman relaxed, flexing his shoulder blades against the pillows. "No one is looking for me," he marveled, delight spreading over him like butter on hotcakes. "I can go back and get the money."

Davy laughed, and Sherman joined in. When they'd finished a good long chuckle, Davy sprang up from the bed and tugged on Sherman's arm.

"Come on, man. Daylight's burning."

Sherman borrowed an old pickup truck from a buddy he'd known since high school. Abiding by every traffic law on the books, he drove down the I-90, watching for the exit he'd taken the night before and navigating the off-ramp like a Sunday driver, even with every nerve throbbing a drumbeat in his veins.

He passed the empty field. The burnt-out husk of the Camry was still in the lane beside it, blackened and deserted, with no sign that anyone had paid it the slightest attention. That was sometimes the way in these rural pockets, Sherman knew.

He cast his eye over the surroundings but saw only a single vehicle coming toward him in the opposite lane. It passed, and Sherman steered the pickup onto the shoulder, executing a three-point turn and heading back.

"Time to get to work," Davy said. "And let's be quick about it before we draw someone's interest."

Sherman had come prepared with gloves and a hand spade. Kneeling in front of the creaking oak, he scraped away the dirt and leaves, exposing the rock. Davy helped him dislodge it, grunting with the effort, and they stared at the bags of cash still resting right where they'd stuffed them in the dark of night.

"Yeah baby, we're rich!"

Davy tugged a bag from the hollow and Sherman reached in for the remaining two. Within minutes, they were back on the freeway, heading west, with the money stashed securely on the floorboard beneath Davy's feet.

Back in the motel room, Sherman placed the three bags in his bed. Sliding beneath the covers, he curled himself around them and slept for a solid eight hours while Davy kept watch.

Sherman's stomach woke him, growling angrily at his neglect. Giving the money bags an affectionate squeeze, he rolled out of bed and grabbed a quick shower. He transferred five twenty-dollar bills from one of the sacks to his wallet and stashed the rest of the cash inside the laundry hamper in his closet, covering them with a layer of dirty clothes.

"Let's get something to eat," he told Davy.

They went to his favorite diner around the corner and took a booth next to the counter. Feeling expansive, Sherman ordered a burger with the works, onion rings on the side and a strawberry malt.

As he dipped the rings in ranch dressing, enjoying the greasy goodness, two cops came through the door. Both swept a gaze over the tables and chairs, examining the customers.

Sherman froze.

He'd seen lawmen do this a dozen times before. It was routine for them to run a quick check with every new venue. He'd heard it called "situational awareness," and it amounted to mentally cataloguing the layout and the people within it. Not really a cause for concern.

Unless you were guilty of something.

"Take it easy, Sherm," Davy muttered.

Sherman swallowed the bit of battered onion sitting on his tongue. The policemen sauntered casually to the counter, taking a couple of stools not far from where he sat, greasy-fingered and uneasy. Sally, the waitress, poured coffee and pushed a saucer filled with creamer capsules between them.

Sherman left his burger half-eaten and slurped the rest of his strawberry shake, signaling Sally for the check. She brought it on a little brown plastic tray and Sherman pulled a twenty from his wallet, placing it on top.

"Keep the change," he told her.

Wiping his fingers on a paper napkin, he rose to leave. One of the cops stirred sugar into his coffee, saying, "Yeah, but here's the thing—those bills are marked. Some luckless son-of-a-gun is going to find that cash and think he's fallen into a bowl of cherries."

ALWAYS GONNA HAPPEN

Sherman paused, helping himself to a toothpick from a dispenser on the counter, listening hard.

The other cop chuckled, blowing across the top of his coffee cup. "Poor sucker'll go on a spending spree and end up in a courtroom, charged as an accomplice in the robbery."

"Sure as bears take a dump in the woods. He should save himself the grief and just turn the money in."

A grunt. "Like that would happen."

Sherman caught Sally at the register, his twenty in her hand. He snatched it back. "Sorry," he mumbled, feeling his face go red. "Can I put that on a card instead?"

Outside the diner, Sherman pinched the bridge of his nose, hoping to ward off the headache pressing down on him.

Davy stood beside him, shuffling his feet on the sidewalk like he always did when agitated. "Nuts!" he said. "We should've just left the cash in the car and burned it all to hell in the first place."

Glumly, Sherman agreed. "Much as I hate to say it, that has to be our next course of action."

Davy sighed. "I guess it was always gonna happen."

He still had his buddy's pickup truck, so he shoved the bags of bills back onto the floorboards. With a vicious yank, he shifted into gear and drove to a nearby lakeside campground. The day was gray and overcast, the site deserted.

Sherman parked the truck in a spot with a stone-encircled fire pit. He gathered enough deadfall and kindling to make a fire and added handfuls of crumpled banknotes to get the whole thing started. He lit the paper, watching tongues of flame lick around the edges and flare to life.

It hurt.

Bundle by bundle, he fed the fire. It was full dark by the time he finished burning the last of the bills. Heart heavy, he trudged back to the pickup truck. Davy walked beside him but, for once, had nothing to say.

He drove to his buddy's and dropped off the truck. He had two choices now to get back to his motel room. Wait around and ride the bus.

Or steal a car.

He walked the street, making sure no one watched as he tried car doors, hoping to find one unlocked. He knew myriad ways to break into a car, but he considered finding one open like a sign.

"Yeah, and how did that work out for you last time?" Davy reminded him.

Sherman decided to take the bus. At the central station, he realized he didn't have the exact change required for the fare to get him home. He got in line for the change machine, watching the bustle of activity around him and taking note of the surveillance cameras placed in strategic positions.

Good thing he now had nothing to worry about.

He got his change and boarded the bus, feeding his two dollars into the slot beside the driver and taking a seat near the rear doors, next to Davy.

"Hey," Davy said. "Where'd you get the singles, wise guy? When you left the motel, all you had was twenties."

Sherman stared at Davy, a hard, heavy rock growing in his gut as he realized his monumentally stupid mistake.

"Aargh! There is no way I'm going back to Monroe for the sake of a crappy twenty-dollar bill!"

Jumping off the bus, Sherman let his gaze

wander over the lot of parked cars. He chose a candy apple red BMW and worked his magic, sliding behind the wheel and firing the engine.

It felt good.

"Yeah, baby. Let's go!" shouted Davy.

Sherman shifted into drive and squealed out of the parking lot, leaving a stripe of rubber on the pavement behind him.

In his cell at the Monroe Correctional Complex for Men, Sherman stretched out on his bunk and stared at the ceiling. Davy sprawled beside him, humming tunelessly.

"Don't feel bad, Sherm. It was always gonna happen."

Sherman didn't feel bad. He felt rotten. Miserable. He really thought he could've done it that time. He could've stayed out.

"Hey, Squirm!"

One of the inmates, a guy called Trashcan because he ate whatever anyone else didn't want, was shouting and waving toward the prison rec room.

"You're on TV, gorgeous," he said. "They're playing your story. Again."

"Yeah, so what?" Sherman said.

Davy stirred on the bunk beside him. "Come on, Sherm. Let's go see what they're saying now."

Grumbling, Sherman pushed himself off the bed and followed Davy into the rec room. A morning talk show played on the TV while footage of the robbery rolled behind the discussion panel. Sherman's face flashed onto the screen, and someone cranked the volume up.

A woman interviewer was asking questions of the guest, a distinguished-looking gentleman in suit and tie. A lawyer, Sherman guessed.

"Funny thing is," the lawyer was saying, "there's only a five-year statute of limitations on bank robbery. All the guy had to do was sit on the cash for a few years and then he could have spent it at his leisure. No one would even be watching anymore for those bills to circulate."

The man said more, but Sherman couldn't hear him above the roar of blood in his ears and the hoots of derisive laughter from his fellow inmates. Mortified, trembling, he stared at Davy.

"I could have been rich," he said. "I could have stashed the cash and put in another five years washing dishes at Antonio's. And then, I could have been rich."

Davy stared back, sadness in his eyes. He shook his head. "No," he said. "You wouldn't have lasted five years with that money burning a hole in your laundry hamper. You'd have stolen your next car before the first year went up in smoke."

"No, I could have done it," Sherman insisted. "You're the one keeps telling me it was always gonna happen. Why not this, then? It could've happened."

Someone slapped Sherman on the back. Hard. Scornful and sarcastic comments flew so thick in the air around him that he barely heard Davy's response.

"Nah, Sherm," his friend told him. "It was never gonna happen."

SATURDAY NIGHT SPECIAL

MICHELE LANG

The minute I saw Emilio coming through my front door I knew I was a dead man.

He held his bolt cutters in his left hand and a tire iron in his right. Saturday night, way after nine o'clock...I knew he wasn't coming to my auto repair shop with a busted carburetor.

Which one was he going to use on me first? The tire iron? Or the cutters?

He smiled as he walked into my office on Jerome Avenue. The door to the storeroom open to my right. My guard dog, Libby, was asleep in there...tied up good on her leash. I'd thought the huge padlocks on the parking lot gate would keep me safe. Wrong.

There was no safe, on Jerome Avenue in the Bronx, in 1978.

"Hola," I said. We spoke in Spanish, the language of the lost motherland, of Cuba.

Emilio smiled, and I knew he wanted me to suffer for a freaking long time before he made me dead. I glanced down at my feet.

My little daughter, Alicia, fit into the hidden space under the desk by my legs...she was only four and there was plenty of room down there for her.

She spent lots of time in her secret spot, watching the shoes of my customers walking in and out of my office. Looking for spark plugs, metallic paint, or...other things. Sometimes, looking to get rid of things that needed to disappear. Cars, certain items, people.

You see, one thing I learned as a boy in Cuba, when times are bad people need things very badly. And if you can supply those things, you will never starve.

I never starved.

Times were hard on Jerome Avenue. So Alicia was used to all kinds of people coming into my shop, in search of all kinds of things, far beyond auto repair supplies. She knew to be quiet. Good thing. Because if Emilio figured out she was under there...

"Let me see your hands," Emilio said, his smile turning into a death mask. He thought I was looking for a weapon under there, a baseball bat or something. Good.

"No problem," I replied, and I tried like hell to smile back. He wasn't here to kill me...I got that now. He wanted something from me, and if I didn't give it to him, or maybe even if I did, then I was dead. But not yet.

I scanned his face, looking for a hint of what was going on in his mind. A tic twitched above his left eyebrow. His smile got twitchy too and I could smell the fear rolling off of him like fog.

I pressed my hands palm down on my desk blotter. "I got some nice cigars, from the old country," I said. "Lemme give you one."

He squinted, trying to reason out my game.

"Come on, man," I said, trying not to sound whiny or desperate. "When was the last time you got to put your lips around a Cohiba Cubatabaco, 'for the people who matter'?"

Alicia shifted under my feet. She could sense my panic, and also that I needed her to stay calm and above all silent.

Far away, a fire truck screamed in the night, raced somewhere else to help somebody else. Not here, not in the South Bronx. Not on Jerome Avenue, where the tenements burned every hot summer Saturday night and the fire trucks arrived too late, if ever.

Me and Alicia were on our own.

"We need to talk," Emilio said, not acknowledging my offer. He squinted and took another step toward me with the tire iron swinging in his right hand, his business hand.

"Anytime," I replied. The sweat slicked down the side of my face, down the back of my neck. But I never took my eyes off the man with the tire iron. Standing a foot away from where my daughter crouched, silent, hidden.

"Martinez sent me," he said.

So that was what was going on. I relaxed a tiny fraction, since even the knowledge of very bad news was better than just not knowing at all. I allowed myself to lean back a little in my creaky chair, to take a deep breath and inhale the fumes of motor oil and auto buffer.

"You want a payout," I said, tired of the game Emilio was playing.

Little fingers played along the cuffs of my pants. Alicia.

I tasted bile in the back of my throat. Emilio worked for the local City Councilman, crooked as Emilio's nicotine-stained teeth. Small time. I knew that if I gave in to Emilio, next would come the guy who worked for the union, then the cops. Then the Mafia. By the time they were done, my skeleton would be picked clean.

I didn't escape from Cuba for this. Guys like Emilio ran my native land. I was damned if I was going to knuckle under to him here, in the free country of the US.

I thought of my sweetheart, Marisol, waiting for me on the fire escape at our apartment in Union City, drinking her glass of wine and squinting up at the stars, obscured by a blanket of smog. Waiting for us to come home. No way was she going to come looking for me here, find the door open, find Alicia and me...

No.

"Why you coming now?" My voice sounded stronger, more assured.

"Because you making money now," Emilio said. "We was watching, knowing that in the beginning, you didn't need our services. But now..."

Alicia found the revolver tucked into my ankle holster. Must've yelled at her a million times never to touch a gun, never never. She unsnapped the holster, put her tiny hands around the butt of the gun.

"Now I need some protection," he said.

I nodded. "Well, yes."

Now that we were having a conversation, Emilio relaxed, thinking that I was doing all the work for him. "The Bronx ain't no Union City, Cuba town jive. This is New York. Big time. And you get in big trouble here if you don't make friends with the right people."

Alicia hesitated, the gun heavy in her little hands. I held my breath, knowing that if I even glanced down Emilio would get distracted, suspicious.

"So Martinez is big time? What can he do for me?"

His face hardened and I knew I'd pushed Emilio too far. He took another couple of steps and now he was standing right on the other side of the desk. The bolt cutter dangled about six inches from the back of Alicia's skull.

She slipped the gun into my lap. Saturday Night Special, numbers filed off, fully loaded, ready for anything.

"That's not the question," Emilio said. "You pay up, you find out the details. You don't..."

He lifted the tire iron.

A low snarl rose from the store room and Libby, my German Shepherd, slipped her choke chain and lunged for Emilio's throat. She had been listening, my girl, my pretty, vicious girl...I'd gotten her from the pound and I swear she had a South American general for her first owner because she was trained to perfection. She'd waited until Emilio made his move, and then she did exactly what I wanted her to do.

Emilio didn't stand still. He swung that tire iron around but Libby sunk her jaws into his left arm before he could connect, He hit her, but the force of his blow got blunted by the momentum of Libby's attack.

Emilio howled and shrieked, and Libby shook his forearm like a chew toy. She didn't bother growling or yelping out in pain as he hit her with the iron, she just dug deeper.

I leaped over the top of my desk and grabbed Emilio by the throat. This close, I could smell his blood.

"Dear heart," I whispered in his ear. I took the pistol and lifted it up, high enough to get into his line of sight. His eyes widened but between me and Libby Emilio wasn't going anywhere now.

"Drop it," I said, louder. Emilio dropped the tire iron and the cutters.

I jammed the working end of the gun under his jaw, next to where I held him in a choke hold. By now, I was pumped up to shoot the bastard, kill him dead like he deserved. The cops wouldn't care...clear case of self-defense, especially once they saw my daughter at the scene.

But Martinez...he would care. He would care and care until I was also dead. And when he found out about Alicia...

Reluctantly, I loosened my hold. "Get out of here. Don't ever come back, Emilio, not unless you want to die."

Libby worried his forearm some more. "Let it go, girl," I said.

She glanced at me, clearly annoyed she wasn't going to get the chance to rip the guy's arm off. Libby let him go, and I swear she sighed as she did it.

Emilio staggered backward, his face green pale now. "You stupid whore, you are going to bite it," he snarled. He knelt to pick up his tools. And he backed his way all the way out of my auto repair shop and onto the street.

I watched him slam out the door, already regretting the fact I'd let him live. But then I heard Alicia's husky little voice, barely above a whisper. "Papi?"

No. I'd done the right thing. But there was gonna be hell to pay for it.

I had to get to Marisol right away, before anybody else did. I got Alicia into the car, left Libby to guard the place, and we peeled out of the parking lot and down the Cross Bronx toward New Jersey.

I had a war on my hands, now. To fight a war, you need allies. As I unlocked the door to our apartment, I thought about how much Marisol had to know, to fight this war with me.

What I didn't expect was the suitcase on the

bed, half-filled with clothes. Marisol fully dressed in street clothes, not her welcome home night clothes.

The look on her face told me more than I wanted to know.

"You're back early," she finally said.

I crossed my arms across my chest and glanced at Alicia. I could see her shaking from across the room. My heart pounded like war drums.

"Where are you going?" I kept my voice calm, but Alicia whimpered. She was more unsettled than back at the shop with Emilio.

Marisol looked away, swiped at the corners of her eyes with the back of her hand. She shrugged. "I miss my family. I miss...everything."

It dawned on me that, no, she wasn't betraying me, not exactly. But I couldn't get the meaning of her words to sink in and make any kind of sense.

I missed Cuba too...the baking hot sun, the jewel colors of the ocean, my uncles and my own brother, who chose to stay behind. But I understood that the Cuba I knew as a child was dead. Maybe Marisol refused to see it.

I couldn't believe it. But I tried to.

Finally, I choked out the words. "You want to go back? To Cuba? Are you out of your mind?"

I spit the words, like they tasted of poison. They actually kind of did.

She looked me right in the eyes, pinned me. "It's too hard. I…"

She didn't want to say it. How she was even more afraid here than she had been in Havana. How the things I was doing to keep us alive were making her want to die.

We never spoke about it. We never agreed I would take the kind of chances I was taking. But I'd always thought she trusted me to keep her safe.

I had let her down. In so many ways.

"My heart…" I murmured, and I gathered my woman into my arms. Her scent intoxicated me like it always did, my favorite drug. "Don't be afraid. Don't run away from me."

She took a deep, shuddering breath, then relaxed into my embrace.

"Papi."

I looked down and Alicia was looking up at me, her dark eyes wide. She looked solemn, ancient.

"I heard a car door slam down on the street."

That girl had the ears of a little alley cat. We were on the fourth floor and Marisol had shut and locked up the windows.

"Shush," I said, forcing my voice calm. I took

a deep breath, inhaled the perfume of Marisol's hair, her skin. Another car door slammed, so faint that even straining to listen I barely heard it.

That meant there was more than one man.

"We need to go now," I said, as gently as I could.

Marisol sighed, shook her head. "No," she said.

"You don't understand."

She shook her head some more. "I'm tired of looking over my shoulder, tired of running."

"I know." I led her to the window, the fire escape.

"I can't do this."

"I know." I opened the window, nodded for Alicia to climb out.

The breeze tickled the top of my head...the night air had cooled off a lot. I looked up, but the glare from the streetlights hid the stars.

I dared to poke my head out the window, still holding Marisol in my arms. Just in time to see two dudes slamming through the apartment building's front door.

I squeezed Marisol gently, then let go and slid onto the fire escape. "Now your turn."

We looked at each other. The elevator was

busted so I knew we had a couple of minutes but that was it.

Marisol's eyes filled with tears.

"We can talk about it later, sweetheart. Let's go."

She nodded and half sighed, half hiccupped. Marisol swung her hips over the windowpane and onto the fire escape.

I looked down again. If we timed this right, we'd get away clean.

"You carry Alicia," I said. "Go first."

The rusty metal ladder swayed under our feet, and I silently cursed our cheap-ass landlord. One floor down, three more to go.

I heard yelling from the open window above our heads. The white curtains billowed out the window looking like trapped ghosts...I should have closed the window from the outside before we left, to hide our escape path.

I expected bullets now. Started taking the steps down faster and faster.

Damn ladder I was on was rusted all the way through.

Foot went right through the middle of the chicken wire on the step.

Marisol caught the scream trying to climb out of her throat. She'd been through too much already, and she knew too well how bad a scenario like this could turn out. We'd both seen our share of dead bodies, both here and back home.

Damn it. I shook my head even as I tried to yank my foot out of the busted step. I still thought of Cuba as home, just like Marisol. No matter how much I wanted to turn my back and face the future.

Some pissed-off yelling from the guy hanging out my window, something garbled up in English. My English is good, but that guy was speaking in tongues.

The side table from our bedroom slammed out of the window and missed my left ear by about an inch. The wind blew into my eardrum as the pointy metal legs whished past my jaw.

No shooting. So, they still didn't want to kill me, then, not exactly. But they were going to mess me up if they got to me.

And the girls…

I yanked my converse sneaker off my right foot to get clear of the rusted metal step. Watched it fall and hit the sidewalk under our feet.

"Go, Marisol, go faster," I said, an edge of panic creeping into my voice.

She shot me a sharp look. "Right now, I'm staying close to the guy with the gun." She glanced at my ankle holster and wiggled her eyebrows at me. I knew she hated that gun, thought about it all the time.

It was still loaded. Ready to go.

I was tired of running, too. But right now we had the choice of running or getting fucked up. To me, the choice was clear.

The ladder creaked and protested as we inched down. My palms were coated in rust off the railings. We had to get away, fast.

But I had a death wish, a need to know.

Who the hell was throwing my bedroom contents out of my window? I paused and looked up, like the lady in the Bible looking over her shoulder while Sodom got destroyed.

The guy leaned out my window, holding my T.V. It was so enormous that I marveled at the upper body strength the guy had, even as he aimed the T.V. at my head.

Mother of God.

I looked at the guy, the guy looked at me. And we got frozen in time.

I couldn't believe it.

It was my brother. My own brother.

I last saw him in Havana.

Now, I kind of understood why that lady got

turned into a pillar of salt. Sometimes looking backwards really is fatal.

"Horacio!" I yelled. "Welcome to America!"

He dropped the TV. Not aimed at my head, which was why I lived to see the next moment of my life. It smashed on the sidewalk and my little girl Alicia finally had enough. She screamed and buried her face into the crook of Marisol's neck.

"It's you," he finally said, gaping.

"Don't let your brains fall out," I said, quoting my father. I started laughing hysterically, the kind of laughing that makes you throw up if you don't quit it.

I pulled myself together, then shot a look at Marisol. She looked up, shook her head. Then, without saying anything, she took off for the street level with Alicia. Smart girl…she understood that sometimes, even standing near the guy with the gun isn't always the safest option.

I looked down at my abandoned sneaker, lying all alone on the sidewalk twelve feet under me. I gripped the rusty rungs of the fire escape ladder.

Then started climbing up.

Horacio watched me coming. He didn't run away, didn't swing a tire iron around like a crazed gorilla, the way Emilio did back at the shop. I think he didn't know how to react to the sight of me.

It was my guess that he didn't know the guy he was supposed to terrorize was in fact his own brother. And that made for some pretty interesting implications.

Out of breath, I finally reached my bedroom window. Deep shadows cast by the moonlight played over my brother's face.

"What are you doing?" I finally asked.

My little brother was loyal. He was strong as a tank. However, he wasn't smart. He used to lean on me, back in the day. But now...

"Following orders," he said. His voice was saturated with regret.

"You know you sound like a thug, right?"

He shrugged his mountain shoulders and sighed. "Ain't no easy life," he said.

"When did you get here? Did you visit Papi yet?"

He shot me a hurt, furtive look. Like a beat down dog. Jesus.

"Who you working for? Why you acting like such an idiot?"

The hurt turned to hot fury. Horacio's eyebrows slammed down his wrinkled forehead. The rage of a true musclehead. Holy Mother.

"They told me you was dead," he said.

"Who told you?"

He hesitated, planted his meaty hands on the windowsill. "The Brotherhood."

I got dizzy then, didn't fall only because I consciously told myself to hang on to the ladder like death.

The Brotherhood. Those guys smuggled you out of Cuba. If you were connected. If you paid the price.

It was a high price.

"What you messing with those guys?" I asked. "We woulda got you out."

His face darkened in his misery, like he was sinking under water. "Not after you left. No way was they going to let me out of Cuba. No way. They was watching me, every minute...following me. I got on the wrong side. All because you left when you did. How you did."

I swallowed hard. My arms were getting pretty damn tired, hanging off the rotten rusty ladder. "Let me go, and I'll pretend we never saw each other. Okay? I won't say a word to Papi neither."

Horacio's eyes flooded with tears. Always wore his heart on his sleeve, poor bastard. "You are in deeper shit than I am."

My heart sank. I knew it, but hearing him say

it, I really knew it. "How did I piss off the Brotherhood?"

"Emilio. He works for them. The job with the city guy is nothing."

I should have known. Nothing was ever simple in the South Bronx. I should have kept my head down and stayed in the small time, in Union City. But it was the American Dream, you know? You gotta take a risk to get ahead.

I was breaking all kinds of rules, crossing all kinds of lines. Not even realizing how bad I was pissing off the players until it was too late.

I sighed, swayed on the ladder. Sweat made my hands slippery.

"I'm getting out of here, Horacio. You dig that? And you can tell them I got away and then it's their problem."

"I can't do that. They'll kill me."

"So what are you going to do?"

"They said to bring you back alive. But I swear I didn't know it was you!"

I climbed back onto the fire escape landing to give my arms a rest. Between the devil and the deep blue sea now. Horacio, or the blind drop four stories down. I could try to make a run for it, but I couldn't account for the second guy. Was he still in my apartment? Back on the street? Did he have Marisol?

My arms were still shaking.

Saturday night. Good times, good times.

"You want a beer?" This was my last chance, my last try. "We can go somewhere, nobody knows either of us. We can try to figure something out together. Like brothers."

My ankle itched under the holster, from the sweat and also from all the rubbing of the leather against my bare skin. The dungarees I wore covered up the rig, and I guessed that Horacio hadn't noticed it.

I kept my hands where my brother could see them. And considered the odds of this meeting being random.

They were just too long.

The truth has a bitter taste.

"You knew it was me," I said, under my breath.

"No way." But he glanced away, just long enough for me to know this was no crazy New York coincidence.

The world was just too small, sometimes.

"I didn't come for you, okay." he said, after a long, horrible pause.

Jesus. My strength left me then.

No way. I knew what he was going to say. "Marisol."

He met my gaze. Didn't say anything. Didn't have to.

The Brotherhood could smuggle people both ways, I guess.

I stood up, leaned over the fire escape railing looking for her. Long gone. With Alicia.

Shit.

When I looked at him, he had crossed his meaty arms across his chest. But I could tell he felt bad for me.

I felt pretty bad for me, too.

"Look, we had a baby together, little girl name Alicia. Let Marisol go, okay. But not my little girl. That's just cold."

He looked down, shook his head. "Emilio was supposed to keep you occupied while Marisol left alone. You was supposed to do the right thing and pay up, not maul the shit out of him with your Nazi dog."

I thought fast. The moon stared down at me through the smog like a single, accusing eye. "Give me up then. Come on. If the only way I see Alicia is by going with you, then take me."

"Naw. Jesus, just run away. I'll throw an

icebox or something after you and then I can say you got away clean."

"No. Take me in, Horacio. Or I'll find them anyway and tell them you got soft when it counted."

He sighed, rolled his eyes. Reached out a big square hand, hauled me back through the window.

"Jesus Christ. You a huge pain in my ass, brother. Come on, they waiting for me downstairs. They be pissed when they see it's you and not her."

I held my breath hoping Marisol would be in the car. No luck. Just another guy waiting for us on the sidewalk, some guy I mercifully didn't know.

He looked at me, then looked at Horacio. "This the guy?" He sounded surprised. "Where's the girl?"

The car was a Crown Victoria, crappy paint job, rusted out grille. Obviously a chop shop product, a Frankenstein of parts glued together from a bunch of stolen cars. I sighed. It was my job in the Bronx, to make boosted cars clean again. But I took no joy in it.

In Cuba, keeping old cars alive is an art. Here, it was just another form of thuggishness.

"God bless America," I said, my voice dripping with sarcasm.

My brother and the guy just looked at me. The stranger looked like he was seriously considering the possibility of punching all the teeth out of my face.

Horacio shot him a glance. "Don't worry, he's gonna be a good boy now. But she was already gone."

The guy pursed his lips, like he'd just taken a shot glass full of gasoline.

Before he could react, Horacio grabbed me by the elbow, held on to me a little too hard. The unknown guy shook his head, hopped behind the wheel, and I got stuffed into the back seat. The cab of the chop shop car smelled like puke and grass and fear. Nice.

We took off with a squeal of burned rubber and we headed up Bergen Boulevard on the Jersey side to the George Washington Bridge, headed back to the Bronx.

This time of night, the highway was deserted, and aside from the hookers working the rest stop right before the bridge, no sign of life at all.

I contemplated the marshy garbage-festooned

ditch near the rest stop, wondered if that was where I was going to end up.

Nope. We got on the bridge instead of disturbing the blow-job hookers. The stranger drove fast, accurate, and lethal. Wouldn't want to get into a fight with the guy...he was efficient in all of his moves.

I distracted myself with thoughts of him, instead of letting myself dwell on Marisol. What the hell. Every time my mind turned to her, pain knifed me in the guts. I had to keep my focus on the danger at hand, instead of the girl who stole my heart and sold it, like a fence, for the highest street price.

We swung off the lower level of the bridge and onto the Cross Bronx Expressway. So full of potholes it was like riding across the back of a giant's washboard. Damn springs were shot on this crapmobile. All the bouncing was breaking my back.

I didn't flinch, didn't blink. Didn't even glance at my own brother. The time for pain, for bargaining, for contemplation, was over. I was in the kill zone now.

Only been there a couple of times in my life before, kill or be killed. When you go there, time slows down. Every sense gets turned up to maximum, every second of life is like a final taste.

"Slow it down," Horacio protested. "You gonna bust the universal."

"I know what I'm doing," the guy replied. "We late."

Instead of easing off, the guy put the leadfoot down. The Crown Vic started leaping like an orca playing in the waves. Horacio held onto the leather strap over his head, but he was too big to keep still and he kept slopping over to my side of the back seat. I could smell the fear on him when he rolled on me.

I braced myself against the back of the front passenger seat with my knees. Ready to make a move first chance I got. Horacio was stupid not to pat me down or tie me up.

The car shimmied and shuddered, and the rear wheels rumbled as we swerved across the highway.

He busted the axle. I heard it go.

Fear is a funny thing, like a water pipe that breaks in your house, right? It comes out far from the source, flowing through the path of least resistance.

I was obsessed about the undercarriage of this car, the condition of the shocks and the brakes. Like if the car died, I had a better chance. I wanted that mofo car to die...just not quite yet.

The brakes squealed as the effective-looking guy in the front seat tried to maintain control. Bam. The universal joint. Now, the car just revved up, no go.

We were stuck in the middle lane of the Cross Bronx Expressway, I figured at about 2 A.M. on a hot New York City Saturday night. Seriously in deep shit.

It was the whitebread suburban nightmare. The next thing that was supposed to happen was zombies were supposed to come pouring out of the burned out tenements lined up on either side of the highway. The whitebreads had a point.

Lots of cars broke down on that highway, lots of gangs looking to keep their turf. A car has a lot of good parts on it, worth a lot of money. And usually the people inside have less defense on them than the gangs.

So I wasn't surprised to see a group of guys on the overpass point at the busted ass car, then disappear down the stairs to the service road.

It was time to go. I grabbed my gun and pulled up the door lock in one movement. Shoved the door open with my shoulder and rolled out onto the potholed highway.

The driver yelled, and Horacio lunged for me but missed. I slammed the door shut behind me with the foot that had the sneaker on it. And then I hid behind the car before the gang guys could see me on the road. My chances against the gang were way better than with the guy in the front seat.

The guys from the overpass spilled onto the highway from the exit ramp. I strained to see their gang colors, their jackets. It would make a big difference, who was coming to get us. But the streetlights were busted out here, and the only light was from the car's headlights and the moon.

Under the overpass, mixed in with all the graffiti, there was a shrine to somebody who had smashed into the wall. And the stripped hulk of the car still there. Hopefully they at least got the dead body out of there. Man. South Bronx.

I didn't want a shrine to me on the Cross Bronx Expressway. I rolled under the broke car... with a busted universal it wasn't going anywhere after tonight. It was so dark I counted on the gang guys not seeing me.

Half of dozen of them, with switchblades already out. One dude with a machete. That made me think they were a Latin gang, which was good news for us. I squinted, looking for their colors again.

The Demented Maniacs. They were sick bastards, but they didn't hate other races. Anybody could join them, as long as they didn't mind burning, looting, and killing when the time was right. Open minded.

So you could reason with them. They might take the car and leave us alone, especially when they saw Horacio, his size, and found out they worked for The Brotherhood. No street gang wanted to tangle with big business like that.

My plan was to stay under with the car and start shooting only as a last resort. I'd deal with Horacio and the crafty guy behind the wheel when we'd gotten past these dudes.

"Hola," their leader called, and the other guys with him started catcalling and hooting like we was a bunch of women.

I grinned to myself under the car, halfway to being a demented maniac myself. These guys were about to experience some serious pain if they didn't back off.

Horacio did a stupid thing, got out of the car. He was gigantic, okay, but sometimes that just makes you more of a target. And now he didn't have the car as armor, the way I still did.

He started talking in rapid-fire Spanish, how they could have the car but they were on official business, not to mess with them.

Totally level-headed talking as far as it went.

But it assumed these kids weren't high, or in an evil-ass mood. Horacio had assumed too much.

The dude with the machete stepped forward, laughing like a demon. The guy was stoked on something nasty...I was guessing angel dust cut with rat poison, something that rotted his brain. He brandished the blade over his head, screaming something incoherent.

Before he brought the machete down on Horacio's skull, I fired. Hard to get a decent shot...I aimed for the heart, but I got him in the head. Not pretty, but effective.

He went down, and then we had a fight on our hands.

Not good, three against five now. But we were three tough old bastards who had survived a lot of bad shit, whereas our opponents were young, hopped up on junk, and stupid.

Horacio held out his hands, screaming, still trying to negotiate. My brother was always a dreamer.

With a sigh, I rolled out from under the car, again with the car between me and the gang. And I started shooting again...in the heat of the battle, I don't think they ever realized I was actually there.

The skilled guy in the front seat emerged with

his own piece. He pointed it at the guy who had started the whole thing by yelling hello, and that guy was coherent enough to realize that the gun wins over knife at a ten foot distance. He raised his hands, cursed and spat.

Demented Maniacs, still open to reason.

The skilled guy said, "Drop the weapons," and the boys did as they were told, good boys. And then the guy told them to lie down on the highway, hands behind their heads.

A semi rumbled by in the left lane, blasting its horn like crazy. Swooped past us like death, and then it was gone under the overpass.

When I looked back at the gang, the driver had walked across that ten foot distance, pistol cocked. That sick bastard was going to execute those kids on the highway.

I didn't think. Aimed and shot the guy in the back. He went down, screaming, and I ran from behind the car and shot him in the back of the head.

At the time, I cursed myself for a fool the second after I'd done the deed by instinct. But looking back, I did what I had to do.

If he was willing to execute those guys after they dropped their weapons, admitted their defeat, then he would have shot me in the face, no matter what I did to cooperate with his bosses. That was this guy's job, obviously. Only one way to deal with somebody like that.

The kids freaked and I yelled "Get the hell out of here!" and they wisely left their shit on the highway and got out of there.

So it was just me, Horacio, two dead guys and a dead car. On the Cross Bronx Expressway.

"I got three bullets left," I warned him. I wasn't quite right in the head myself by then.

He held up his hands, the big peace maker. "I figure that. You got me. So what you wanna do, shoot me too?"

I realized I was pointing the gun at the center of his mass, and I forced myself to breathe, slow down a little.

"I'll tell you what I want," I finally said. "I want my little girl with me, not going back to Cuba with Marisol."

Horacio wrinkled his forehead. I looked at him, he looked at me. The world closed down into a circle, with just the two of us hidden inside.

"I don't care about nothing anymore. Just get me Alicia, and we're even."

He scratched the back of his head, sighed. "They all waiting back at your shop. How about this…I go in alone, get your little girl for you. Then you and her just go. Okay?"

We both knew what this was going to mean. It was going to be ugly.

"My dog is dead, right?"

Horacio shrugged, didn't answer.

Libby, my vicious, loyal girl. The bastards.

I had more reasons to leave New York now than Marisol did. But I didn't care. I was tired of running, but I'd never look backward again.

I was finished with Cuba.

I held out my left hand…my right hand still gripped the gun. He shook it with his right, with that big, square hand. Still brothers, even now.

We walked together, down the middle of the Cross Bronx Expressway, leaving the mess on the highway behind us. Every so often, souped up Toyota Corollas, beat up white and champagne pink Cadillacs, and the odd Mercedes swerved to keep from hitting us. But we both knew it was safer, in the middle of the highway, than walking the local streets.

One exit until Jerome Avenue. One exit until Alicia. The dream of a future, looking forward, finally free of the past. Numbers filed off, fully loaded, ready to go.

Saturday night in the Bronx.

DODGING BULLETS

DAVID H. HENDRICKSON

If Butchie had ever suspected what was in the trunk, he never would have boosted the Lexus. Wouldn't have come near the damned thing. Treated it like a freaking hazmat site. Like it was oozing Ebola. Made it somebody else's problem. Just kept walking, wearing his plain black T-shirt and jeans, minding his own business.

You didn't get to be a grizzled veteran of the business at the ripe old age of thirty-seven by messing with the wrong people. Even by accident. His brown hair might be thinning and his gut, thickening. Hell, some days it seemed as though his once-impressive rippling chest muscles had crashed into his midsection like an ugly mudslide. And perhaps not so coincidentally, he wasn't quite the hit with the ladies he'd been in years past.

But he could still break into cars at the drop of a hat and get them to Louie's shop with the best of them. Nobody any better. You could start a stopwatch on Butchie and from first move to pounding a celebratory Budweiser with the boys at the shop, he was as fast as ever. Maybe even faster.

Like a fine wine, Butchie liked to think, he was aging quite well, his mudslide of a gut and the disinterested ladies be damned. Getting better with age.

He smiled and licked his lips in anticipation of the cold Budweiser—he didn't give a rat's ass that it was barely eleven in the morning—and pulled the silver Lexus into the shop's middle bay. Behind him, Paulie lowered the garage door with its darkened window, and Butchie hopped out.

Louie's shop, here in this quiet, one-stoplight town less than an hour north of Boston, smelled of grease, rubber, and antifreeze. The overhead lighting glowed brightly, illuminating the three bays, all now filled, though only Paulie's Hyundai on the left was up on its lift. Getting an oil change.

As if this was a legit business. Who'd a thunk it.

"Nice one," Paulie said with an appreciative nod. He was a kid, barely old enough to drink legally, although legal necessities weren't exactly high on the priority list of the boys here. Hell, Paulie had been guzzling beer almost out of the womb, to hear him tell it. As if he'd been getting Budweiser during breastfeeding. Straight out of the tap, so to speak.

A good-looking kid, Paulie, with his jet black hair and the chiseled physique Butchie liked to think had been his own back at that age. A couple inches taller than Butchie, though, maybe six-one. A bit of a smart ass. But clumsy as an ox when it came to boosting a car. Paulie couldn't spot an alarm if you shoved it up his ass or his crooked, oversize nose. And practically wet his pants driving away from the scene, wide eyes almost glued to the rear view mirror, looking for the blue flashing lights and screeching siren of a cop car.

So Paulie was strictly a break-down man. Take the product delivered to him by Butchie or one of the other boys and chop it up into spare parts. Spare parts worth more than the resale of the car. Get it done, depending on the car, in barely more than an hour or two most of the time.

Like clockwork.

Butchie headed for the back room to take a leak and celebrate with a Bud, especially pleasing on this unseasonably warm spring day. He'd barely done the former and only cracked open the latter, however, when Paulie's panic-filled voice called from out front.

"What the hell have you done?" Paulie yelled.

It would have been better if the trunk contained bundles of dynamite. Or a foot-high mound of anthrax. Or nuclear waste from that place in Russia...where was it?...Chernobyl. Yeah, Cher-freaking-nobyl.

Butchie and Paulie stared at the dead body in the open trunk. And not just any body.

Jake McMichael.

Looked a lot like a middle-aged Jack Nicholson. Only with the right side of his head blown off. The eye on the other side—the eye not blown to bits—looking up at them.

Unblinking.

A lot like Butchie and Paulie. Unblinking, as they stared at their worst nightmare.

Jake McMichael. Head of the Cold Corpse Cadavers, the outlaw biker gang that controlled the drug and prostitution trade throughout Boston's North Shore.

Now, though, the *former* head of the Cold Corpse Cadavers.

An unwanted correction came from a suddenly ill part of Butchie's brain. *Half* the former head of the Cold Corpse Cadavers.

Butchie couldn't tear his eyes away from what was left of McMichael's face. Pale and bloodless.

Rigid. And that one remaining eye, open and staring at him.

The stench of McMichael's voided bowels and urine hit Butchie like a wet slap. The shock of seeing the dead body—especially its terrifying identity—had delayed Butchie's reaction to the godawful smell, but it revolted him now. Not the ghastly odor of decomposition. McMichael did not appear to have been dead for that long, though Hell would freeze over before Butchie touched the corpse to make sure. He didn't really care how long the body had been dead. Only that somehow it had gotten dumped on him.

The name of the outlaw biker gang, Cold Corpse Cadavers, had suddenly morphed from intimidating to eerily spooky. Terrifyingly so.

"What the hell, what the hell, what the hell," Paulie said, over and over, rapid fire like an auctioneer.

Butchie just stared. Unable to speak. To swallow. To move.

I'm a dead man. Dead as...McMichael.

Butchie's mouth and the back of his throat tasted sour and raw. His gut heaved. His eyes couldn't pull away from that one wide-open, dead eye of Jake McMichael staring at him.

Accusing Butchie.

As if he'd pulled the trigger, killing one of the most feared men north of Boston. Then dumped the dead body in there.

"I ain't no murderer," Butchie blurted out.

"Hit man," Paulie said, correcting Butchie, always the smart ass. Pouring gasoline on the freaking fire inside Butchie's brain.

"I didn't know he was in there," Butchie protested. "How was I to know? It was just a car. A freaking Lexus. Almost new. I thought he drove a Maserati."

"He does," Paulie said. "At least when he ain't riding his Harley. New Maserati. Not even a year old. This ain't his car."

Butchie stared at the blown-off, right side of Jake McMichael's bloodless head. And the lone eye staring up at him.

"But it sure is his body," Butchie said, wishing it weren't true.

"No shit, Sherlock," Paulie said, then added, "What's left of it."

More gasoline on the fire.

"So whose car is it?" Butchie asked, his fevered mind racing every which way. "Just some random stolen car used to dump the body?"

"Stolen twice," Paulie said.

"What?"

"Stolen twice, if that's what happened," Paulie said. "Hitman stole it to dump the body. Then you stole it a second time."

"*Who cares if it was stolen twice?*" Butchie yelled, realizing too late his voice was shrill. Trying without luck to tone it down, he said, "How is that helpful?"

"I was just saying."

"Well, don't!" Butchie snapped. "Maybe it wasn't stolen twice anyway. Could be there's nothing random about it at all. Could be..." Butchie's mind raced. "Could be the car belonged to some target. Maybe the hitman was sending a message. Or trying to pin the hit on someone. Set the owner up for the fall. Get him arrested for murder. Or killed by members of the Cadavers."

Members of the Cadavers!

An icy fist grasped hold of Butchie's heart. He could barely breathe.

Mick!

Mick O'Donnell was due to show up anytime now. Mick, a longtime member of the Cold Corpse Cadavers. The one guy in the shop who wouldn't be able to look the other way, keep his mouth shut, and pretend nothing had happened.

"We gotta get this outta here," Butchie said,

raw terror choking the words. "Right away. Before Mick shows up."

A low, gravelly voice echoed from the back room. "What do you got to get outta here before Mick shows up?"

Butchie's heart almost gave out. For a long instant, Butchie was sure the raspy voice was Mick's. He really was a dead man. No way out.

But shit didn't hit the fan every freaking time. It only seemed that way.

It was Louie standing in the doorway to the back, not Mick, their gravelly voices similar from years of smoking. Louie stood there wearing jeans and a grease-covered wifebeater, the single most unflattering piece of clothing for a man not quite six-feet tall but well over three-hundred pounds. Bald on top with black hair around the side.

Butchie's mouth went dry. The words remained lodged in his throat, so Louie had to repeat himself. "What do you got to get outta here before Mick shows up?"

"Um…" Butchie began, unable to speak the name for a few long seconds before he finally spat it out. "Jake McMichael."

Louie's eyes widened. "The Cadavers' Jake?"

Butchie nodded, realizing his own eyes were as

wide as Louie's. And maybe as unblinking as Jake McMichael's lone one.

"Get that thing out of here!" Louie demanded. "Don't just stand there with your heads up your asses. Get it out of here! Fast! And I don't ever want to hear about it being here! It ain't here now. It never was here. Got it?"

Butchie slammed the trunk shut and headed for the driver's seat, hearing Paulie ask the dumbest question in the world.

"Get rid of the body or the car?" Paulie asked, having apparently tabulated already how much the Lexus parts were worth and what he could spend his share on.

"The whole damned thing!" Louie yelled. "What part of, 'it was never here' don't you understand?"

Butchie glanced in the rear view mirror as the bay door with its darkened window closed behind him. He put on his sunglasses and told himself not to go a single mile over the speed limit of thirty-five. The habit had been ingrained in his mind for as long as he'd been stealing cars for a living. Not since the joyrides of his youth had he broken the rule. Boosting Cars 101, a short-timer college boy at the shop had once called it, flaunting his three drunken years at UMass majoring in Physical Education as if he was a freaking Einstein and Butchie was a dope.

Well, Butchie was no dope. He knew Boosting Cars 101, 201, 301, and 401. Hell, he had his PhfreakingD in Boosting Cars. But driving a stolen car was one thing. Driving a stolen car with a dead body in the trunk was another. And when that dead body was Jake McMichael, the brain got more scrambled than it did after six shots of Jack Daniel's.

So Butchie focused sharply on what was usually instinctive. He drove like he was a grandma, his fingers choking the steering wheel at the ten and two position until his knuckles were white. His eyes locked onto the open road in front of him, tearing them away only for a quick glance at the speedometer every few seconds. He noticed none of the cars parked against the curb along the side of the road. He shut off his peripheral vision after it spotted a sweet young thing walking along the sidewalk. Noticed nothing but what was straight ahead.

Tunnel vision until he got out of this mess.

Sweat trickled down the side of his face. He

ignored it. The armpits on his plain black T-shirt grew increasingly damp. He ignored it. The smell of the dead body in the trunk—its stench of shit and urine—lingered in his nostrils. Or perhaps was even drifting into the Lexus's interior, new and not at all afresh. He tried to ignore it.

Even though it was revolting.

He ignored it for as long as he could, unwilling to give in to any distraction, letting his gut roil as if he were out on the ocean with the waves rocking him back and forth. Finally, though, he had to cry uncle. Had to get some fresh air. Had to get rid of that stench. Allowing himself a split second, he found the window button on the side arm rest and hit it.

Fresh air rushed in.

Butchie gulped the cool, clean air and heaved a sigh of relief. Then returned his laser focus to the road ahead. Oncoming cars approached, but there was no longer any traffic in front of him. It had all left him far behind. Driving only thirty-five miles an hour made him feel painfully conspicuous. Conspicuous as hell. But he didn't care.

Behind him, a car horn honked. Butchie ignored it.

The horn sounded again, this time a long, sonorous *blaaaat*.

Butchie permitted himself a quick glance in the rear view mirror. Traffic had queued up behind him six or more cars deep. Shit! No one actually drove thirty-five miles an hour in a thirty-five mile an hour zone unless they were hiding something. The desire—the obsessive *need*—became almost overpowering to inch that speed up just a crack to not be so obvious, to stop announcing, *Hey look at me, I'm doing something suspicious as hell.*

But Butchie resisted. Just five miles to go. Even if it all was at this brutally slow pace. He wasn't going to give in to temptation. Was going to stick to the plan. Give himself a fighting chance of getting out of this mess alive.

Easier, it turned out, said than done.

He maintained his iron-clad resolve for all of half a mile. With four and a half left, the thunderous roar of motorcycles exploded from behind. Not just one or two. A dozen or maybe more.

Butchie's blood ran cold.

The lead biker pulled up alongside, his Harley roaring its presence through the Butchie's open window. Behind him, the rest of the outlaw posse rode single file, straddling the road's center line and stretching back past the entire queue of cars behind Butchie, pinning them all in if any had been tempted to ignore the solid yellow line and pass.

No one was honking now. The road had become deathly silent except for the thundering Harleys.

Butchie's heart jackhammered. His breath quickened. He throat clenched tight.

This was it. Execution time. All because he'd picked the wrong damned car to steal.

Staring straight ahead, eyes wide, Butchie considered flooring it. He was a sitting duck as it was, just puttering along at grandma speed. But he also couldn't outrun the entire pack of the Cadavers, not through all these winding suburban, almost rural roads, at least not without drawing the attention of every cop in the area. With a dead body in the trunk, stinking to high heaven.

Pick your poison.

He glanced over at the lead biker, a young guy maybe in his early twenties with long blond hair billowing out from beneath his distinctively macabre Cadavers helmet. Butchie checked the rear view and side mirrors and eyed the rest of the outlaw posse. They were all Cold Corpse Cadavers. The ghostly white and purple insignia on their otherwise black helmets and leather jackets left no doubt.

Cold sweat leaked down the back of Butchie's neck and spine. He licked his lips, his foot ready to jam down on the accelerator.

He glanced over again at the long blond-haired lead biker. To Butchie's astonishment, there was no pistol already pointing at him. No extended arm, finger pointing him to the side of the road where he would have to take his medicine. Not even a glare of pissed-off annoyance.

The biker was just staring curiously at Butchie as if he were an odd-looking bug.

Butchie eased the pressure of his foot on the accelerator, not actually slowing down but uncoiling the intended stomping that would have set the Lexus off with a lurch.

"Man, what shit are you on?" the biker yelled.

Butchie opened his mouth but no words came out. He had not been prepared for this. He'd expected anger, fury, and hatred for his perceived role in their leader's demise. And what would follow would be a bullet in the head or a long, slow stomping to death.

An eye for an eye. Not this.

Belatedly, Butchie yelled back, "Great shit!"

and laughed hollowly. "Maybe a little too mellow!"

The biker laughed back. "You gotta wake up and get the lead out, man!"

And then he roared off, followed by the rest of them.

Butchie stared in disbelief. Dodged that bullet! He grinned. Maybe he'd get out of this mess after all.

His grin proved short-lived. Before the Cadavers were even a hundred yards down the road, the car behind honked a long, loud *blaaaat.*

Butchie was pulling the Lexus into the exact parking spot where he'd taken it when the police sirens erupted.

Butchie's heart sank and he almost wet himself. So close and yet so far. He'd escaped the clutches of the Cadavers, at least as far as he could tell. A silver Lexus was hardly a rarity on the roads these days, and though he'd liked to think in past years that he was something special, there were, sad to say, plenty of guys who looked like him. Sloppy and out of shape. Not memorable for the ladies. Not memorable for the Cold Corpse Cadavers.

They'd eventually learn that their leader's body had been found in a Lexus, but if it had not been randomly stolen, someone else would be the target. And if it had been randomly stolen, would the bikers really connect it to the guy driving a Lexus thirty-five miles an hour, five miles away? When only one of them had gotten much of a look at him?

Butchie put it all together and thought he'd dodged every last bullet. The Cadavers weren't going to connect him to their dead boss. He was home free. All that remained was to wipe down the steering wheel and anywhere else in the interior he might have touched, finishing off the wipe-down process Paulie had performed on the exterior, then get the hell out of Dodge without getting noticed.

So close. He'd pulled into the exact same parking spot. So close it was really cruel.

Blue police car flashers pulsed all about him. Sirens screamed. Stick a fork in him. He was done.

Butchie waited for the inevitable.

No bullhorn, however, commanded for him to get out of the car with his hands up. No cop walked up to the Lexus and wrapped on the now-raised window. No cop demanded an explanation for the godawful stench coming from the trunk.

What was happening?

After long, agonizing minutes that felt like hours, during which the sirens pierced Butchie's brain, it began to appear that nothing at all was happening.

The sirens fell silent. The strobing of the blue flashers stopped.

The police cars left.

It had been the worst false alarm of all time. But actually the best false alarm of all time.

Miracles did happen!

Butchie quickly but thoroughly wiped down the interior, looked around to see that the coast was clear, and climbed out of the Lexus.

He took a deep breath, glanced around again, and walked off as if nothing had ever happened.

In a sense, that was perfectly true. The Lexus was exactly where it had been earlier this morning, and the body of Jake McMichael was still untouched. Butchie had dodged a few figurative bullets in the meantime—it felt like he'd dodged an entire round of bullets—but he'd emerged unscathed, not a cent richer or poorer. As if nothing had happened at all.

Some days, that was plenty good enough.

THE ZOMBIE RIDESHARE

ROBERT JESCHONEK

Hands bloody, heart hammering in my chest, I fling open the rear passenger side door of the silver Toyota Camry sedan and dive inside. I still can't believe what I just did or that I got out of the townhouse in one piece...but now I have a decent chance of getting to my next stop before anyone even thinks to come after me.

Thank you, Crimeshare.com. The future of getaways is in the mobile app.

"Go go go!" I slam the door shut and thump the plexiglass divider in front of me with the heel of my hand. "Get me out of here!"

The driver just sits, stiff as the dead body I left in the townhouse. He doesn't twitch, make a sound, or react in any way. Doesn't even ask if I'm Vanessa T., the woman who ordered the ride.

I remember *his* name well enough from the app, though. "Raul!" I beat harder on the divider. "I said *go!*"

Still nothing. The wispy gray hair atop his head flutters in the light breeze from the heater vents...and that's the extent of his range of motion.

Looking over my shoulder, I half expect to see Nicky hard-charging under the lights across the parking lot, pistol in hand, screaming his lungs out about getting revenge on me for killing him.

Never mind he had it coming, ordering the hit on my fiancé Mark—his own fucking *brother*—the way he did. Never mind he planned to kill me, too, when he called me in for a personal audience at two in the morning.

"Raul! Hey!" I really hammer the divider this time. "Are you gonna drive or what?"

Suddenly, the guy's hand shoots over and grabs the gear shift, jerks it from Park to Drive. He yanks the wheel hard, stomps the accelerator, and the car spins away from the curb in a wild U-turn that throws me across the back seat.

SCREEEEEE

"Hey!" My shoulder thuds into the driver side door, sending a white-hot flash of pain through the joint. "What's your *problem*, pal?"

His only reply is to send the car racing up the street at a high rate of speed, slamming me back against the seat so hard it takes my breath away.

That alone, I don't necessarily object to. Getting away from here and across town as fast as possible is what I'm paying this guy for—not to mention paying Crimeshare's steep peak-time fees on top of the base rate. Paying for services in the gig economy can get pretty pricey, especially in the *dark* gig economy.

But the silent treatment is starting to get old...

THE ZOMBIE RIDESHARE

and problematic.

"We're going the wrong way, Raul!" Straightening, I grab the driver-side seat belt and wrench it around in front of me. I plug the hasp into the buckle with a loud click, securing myself just in time for the car to swing around a tight right turn.

At first, I think maybe he's just circling the block to change direction and will end up going the right way. I logged my destination into the app when I ordered the ride, so it makes sense that the route might be recalibrating in his GPS system. There's just one problem.

As I quickly realize, this guy has no GPS system.

Glaring through the divider, I see no video screen on the dash. There *is* a phone mount up there, but no phone on it with a maps app running. In other words, none of the direction-seeking tools used by every rideshare driver or cabbie on the planet these days.

I'll tell you what I *do* see up front, though, and it chills me to the bone.

Raul's eyes in the rearview mirror are halfway rolled up into the sockets of his skull as if he's in a trance.

Those are the eyes of the guy at the wheel of my getaway car right now.

It's sinking in that I've got a problem here. Whatever's going on with the driver, it isn't good…and I don't have time to deal with it.

I need *out*, plain and simple. As soon as the car slows down, assuming it does, I need to throw the door open, jump out, and make a run for it.

At least that's the plan until I give the door handle an experimental tug, and it goes nowhere. I put my back into it, pulling with all my strength… and still, nothing.

"*Child locks*, asshole?" I say it loud enough for him to hear, not expecting a reaction.

He doesn't disappoint. Just keeps driving at breakneck speed through the streets of downtown Pittsburgh, somehow seeing where we're going though his eyes are half-rolled-up in their sockets.

What *is* this guy? Some kind of rain man savant with no communication skills? Or maybe a maniac who uses a cold shoulder routine to build fear in his future victim?

Either way, I can't believe my luck has gone this bad. What are the chances, on a night when I need a getaway rideshare to flee a murder scene, that the app sends *this* freak to be my driver? And here I am without a *gun*, because I wiped mine down and dumped it with Nicky's body back at the townhouse.

Dropping back against the seat, I wipe blood on my black denim jeans and consider the situation. I try to focus on the best case scenario, which is that Raul's silence isn't a danger sign, and he's taking me right where I want to go. If that's the case, the next piece of shit on my list isn't long for this world, and the thought of it does my heart good.

The worst case scenario, though—a painful end for me at the hands of this nut driver—keeps rearing its ugly head. Is Raul capable of such brutality? Is he strong enough to beat me down, as good with violence as I am?

Just as these questions cross my mind, I hear thumping from behind me.

WHUMP WHUMP WHUMP WHUMP

It doesn't take a genius to figure out what that means. The sounds are regular, one after another, not the occasional impacts of something bumped around by the car's wild motion.

And they're coming from the direction of the trunk.

WHUMP WHUMP WHUMP WHUMP

Meaning I'm not the only person trapped in this car.

At first, I almost don't hear the phone ring over the roar of the car's engine and the thumping from behind me. I'm distracted, wondering where Raul is taking me and who the hell he stowed in the Camry's trunk.

But as soon as the ring gets through to me, I scramble to pull the phone from my back pocket. That particular ring tone—the theme from the 1970s *Wonder Woman* TV show—only belongs to one person in *my* world.

"Ange?" I shout her name as I hit the button on the screen to take the call.

"Where the hell *are* you, Vaness?" Ange, my bestie, is shouting, too. "People are *looking* for you, girl."

I don't like the sound of that. "I'm trapped in some guy's car, and I don't know where he's taking me."

"*Seriously?*"

"Yeah, seriously. He won't even *talk* to me."

"How the fuck did *that* happen?"

"Rideshare gone bad." As I say it, the car squeals around a corner, pitching me against the door. Must have pitched whoever's in the trunk, too, because it suddenly goes quiet. "Their driver vetting process *sucks*, if you ask me."

"It's after three in the morning! Where is he *taking* you?"

"Beats the shit outta me," I tell her. "The opposite direction from where I *want* to go is all I know."

"You need to call the *cops*."

"*No cops.*" The words blast out of me before I can tone them down. Given my recent activities, cops are the *last* people I want to see right now... almost. It won't take much for the police to connect me to what happened to Nicky Napolitano, especially if *laughing boy* at the wheel suddenly gets talkative. Then I can kiss my chances of polishing off my *next* target goodbye.

Though the people I'm *most* worried about aren't law enforcement at all. If *they* catch me, I can kiss my *life* goodbye.

"So who's looking for me, Ange?" I ask. "You said *people*."

"*Frankie Beans*, mainly. He called a couple times. Said he's on his way over."

"Shit shit shit." Frankie is the *last* person I want involved in this. If he's in the picture, and he's looking for me, the heat couldn't be any hotter.

Meaning maybe it's for the best my ass is in the wind right now, going God-knows-where with Chatty Cathy at the wheel.

"Don't tell anyone *anything*, Vaness. Promise me."

"But you're in *trouble*." She's usually a toughie, but I hear a tremor in her voice. "If that guy takes you somewhere and *kills* you, I'll never *forgive* myself."

"I'll be fine. I'll figure this out. But you have to *promise* me. Don't say *anything* to *anyone* about this."

"Okay, all right." She sighs. "I promise."

Even as she says it, I wonder how much good it will do. How long will it be until the cops trace my phone, stop the Camry, and haul me in...or hand me over, depending on which cops and who they work for?

Not long enough, I'm guessing.

"Just *trust* me," I tell her. "I can *handle* this."

"At least *call* me," she says. "Let me know you're okay."

"Definitely."

Suddenly, I hear a man's voice shouting—not on the line, but in the trunk. "I've gotta go," I tell Ange as I hang up.

And the man's voice repeats what he said the first time.

"Hey! This is *Raul!* Let me outta this fucking *trunk!*"

Did the real Raul just say what I *thought* he said?

"You mean *he's* not...?" Looking at the driver's half-rolled-up eyes in the rearview mirror, I see no change from before, no flicker of awareness or emotion. "The guy *driving* isn't...?"

"Yeah!" True Raul's voice is muffled by the partition between the back seat and the trunk. "This is *my* fucking *car!*"

"Then who the hell is *driving?*"

He doesn't hear me. "What?"

"Then who's at the *wheel?*" I shout the words as loud as I can. Pretty sure nothing I say will make any difference to the driver.

"He's some fuckin' *dipshit* whose *ass* I'm gonna kick when I get outta here!" Raul thumps around like crazy for a moment, as if to emphasize the severity of his threat.

"Was he one of your fares or what?" I ask when he settles down.

"Just some *douche* standing in the middle of

the *street,* looking *lost.* Reminded me of my granddad with dementia, so I stopped to help... and he pulled a fucking *.38* on me! Pistol-whipped me and threw me in *here,* the asshole!"

My blood turns ice-cold at the mention of a gun. If the driver has one stashed somewhere, the dynamics of this little joyride just turned shittier.

"I was out cold till a few minutes ago," says Raul. "Took a few minutes after that to scrape the duct tape off my mouth...but my arms and legs are a different story. That guy's pretty good at *hogtying* people for someone who acts like they're in a *coma* or something."

"What *is* his *deal*? How can he even *drive,* the state he's in?"

"Fuck if I know!" Raul thumps around some more, then stops. "You got anything up there for cutting *ropes?*"

Reaching into the vest pocket of my black leather jacket, I take hold of the scrolled metal handle of my stiletto...or as I like to call it, "the Nicky sticker."

When I gutshot Nicky and took him down, only to have him revive and grab me from the blood-soaked floor, *this* was what saved my life. *This* was the weapon that sealed the deal.

It's also the only real weapon I have on hand.

THE ZOMBIE RIDESHARE

If phony Raul decides to come for me, this knife might be the only thing that keeps me alive.

Then again, if it gets Real Raul out of the trunk, my chances for survival might improve even more.

"I've got something." I unbuckle my seatbelt and slip the stiletto out of my jacket pocket. "Gonna try pushing it between the seats and through the partition."

"Do it!"

"Just watch out," I tell him as I start driving the blade into the narrow gap between the backrests. "It's coming point-first, and it's sharp as shit."

"Spoken like a true Crimeshare customer!" says Raul. "Remember, client confidentiality applies under our terms of service. I'll never rat you out if you let slip why you have that knife *with you* tonight in the first place."

"Trust me on this, Raul." Gripping the hilt tightly with both hands, I punch the blade through the gap repeatedly, hacking a hole in the pressboard between the cabin and trunk. "You *do not* want to know about this knife."

The phone rings again a few minutes later, as the car begins to slow. I'm done pushing the knife into the trunk by now, and Raul is hacking at his bonds the best he can in the close confines.

Ange's special ringtone plays again....and again. I hesitate to pick up in case Ange has Frankie Beans on the call. On the other hand, it might not be a bad thing to have the line open in case Chatty Cathy pulls that .38 on me.

Just as I'm about to answer, Raul hollers from the trunk. "Where the hell *are* we? Why's the zombie douchebag stopping?"

"No idea." We're in a bad part of town, on a street even a lifelong homegirl like me doesn't recognize. All I see on either side are boarded-up, rundown storefronts that look like they've been vacant for decades. I don't see a single light on in any of them. "Some shithole neighborhood on the North Side."

"Perfect place for an execution and body dump," Raul says darkly. "And I'm still not through *any* of these fucking *ropes.*"

I get nervous as Cathy turns down a dark side street and kills the headlights. That's my cue to finally answer the phone, which has been ringing all this time.

"Vaness, thank God!" Ange sounds even more

worked up than before. "I was starting to think something happened to you!"

"Hey, Ange." I keep my voice low as the Camry rolls to a stop. "Could you hold a minute? We just pulled up somewhere, and I'm not sure what this guy has in mind."

"What do you *mean* you don't know what he..."

"Shh!" For the first time since I got in the car, the driver throws it in Park and opens the door. As he gets out, I see he's stiff as ever...and carrying something in his right hand.

The .38.

"What's happening?" asks Ange.

"What the fuck's going on?" asks Raul.

All I can think about is the gun and what to do about it if he opens my door.

Swinging myself around, I grip the seat hard and draw back my knees, ready to let fly with as much of a two-legged kick as I can muster. Maybe, if I clock him just right, I can throw the bastard back and give myself enough room to leap out and maneuver. Maybe the gun'll even come free within reach, and I can change the dynamic for the better.

"Vaness? Vaness?"

Heart slamming against my ribs, I wait as the

old man closes his door and steps toward mine with gun in hand. I prime myself the best I can, psyching myself up for the coming struggle just as I psyched myself up earlier tonight to handle Nicky.

Then the old man walks on by without even a glance in my direction. Oblivious as always, he suddenly cuts left around the back of the car—then marches across the street toward the burned-out, boarded-up shell of the bar that once existed there.

Huey's Place. That's what the grime-encrusted sign above the front door says, flanked by the logos of two different brands of cheap beer.

"I can't figure this guy out," I say, more for my own benefit than anyone else's. "He's crossing the street, heading for some old, dead bar."

"What bar?"

"Huey's, it says on the sign."

"Never heard of it." Ange sighs. "And you still don't know who he *is?* He's still not *talking?*"

"Not a word."

"You're sure you don't recognize him? Can you get a better look at him now that he's out of the car?"

"If he wasn't facing away from me, maybe." I watch as he marches toward Huey's with the .38

THE ZOMBIE RIDESHARE

hanging at his side. "It's pretty dark out there right now, though. No streetlights or neon signs on this block."

"Here's an idea," says Ange. "Why don't you shoot a *video* with your phone when he comes back toward you? Phone cameras are great in low light these days, and yours is pretty new, isn't it?"

She might be onto something. "Sure." I scoot across the back seat, open the camera app, and raise the phone to the rear passenger side window. "It can't hurt to try."

Turning the phone on its long edge with the camera lens aimed at the street, I pick the video option and hit the red button that starts the recording. The driver hasn't turned around yet, but rolling early might help me avoid last-second technical glitches.

My timing, it turns out, couldn't be better.

"Recording." I follow the driver with the phone, keeping him centered in the frame as best I can. It's dark out there, but Ange was right about the camera's low-light feature; I can still make him out as if it's twilight instead of 3:30 AM as he steps up onto the curb and stands motionless.

"What's *happening* out there?" Raul shouts from the trunk. "What's the douchebag *doing?*"

I'm about to answer when the driver swings up his gun hand.

He's still facing Huey's, pointing the gun in the general direction of the front of the place. I don't see anyone else on the block except him and the two of us in the Camry.

"He's aiming the .38," I say. "But I can't tell what he's aiming it *at*."

"*The .38? He's got a gun?*" yells Ange. "What the actual *fuck*, Vaness?"

Suddenly, the driver pulls the trigger.

KRAKRAKKK

I have to fight to keep the camera roughly on target as I jump at the sound of the bang.

"What the *fuck?*" shouts Raul from the trunk.

"Vaness, are you—" shouts Ange.

And then the driver fires again.

KRAKRAKKK

"Vaness!" howls Ange.

"Don't worry," I tell her. "He isn't shooting at *me*."

KRAKRAKKK

That makes three shots, every one of them fired into thin air—every one of them captured on video.

"What's he *shooting* at?" asks Raul.

THE ZOMBIE RIDESHARE

"Nothing," I tell him and Ange at the same time. "Not a fucking thing that *I* can see."

The driver turns and marches back to the car. I capture his robotic approach on video, from his rigid posture to his half-rolled-up eyes...at least until he rounds the back of the car, passing out of the frame.

I stop recording then in case I need to defend myself, but he goes straight for the front driver-side door. As he hauls it open and slides in behind the wheel, I hastily send the video file to Ange.

"I just texted you the video," I tell her. "Let me know if he looks familiar."

"Because I know so many psycho rideshare jockeys who drive around shooting places up for no reason?"

"Just take a look." As I say it, the car's engine rumbles to life. "And remember, don't tell *anyone* about *any* of this."

"You need to call the cops."

"No cops, and no Frankie Beans," I snap. "You said he was coming over, remember?"

Ange hesitates. "Well, he did...and he's worried about you."

"Bullshit." *I'm* the one worrying because Ange has a soft spot for Frankie, God knows why. "You didn't *tell* him anything, did you?"

Again, Ange pauses. "He told me Nicky Nap is dead."

"Good for him."

"Your dead fiancé's brother," says Ange. "Somebody killed him."

The driver flicks on the headlights, and the car starts rolling. "Ange, I gotta go. We're back on the move."

Again with the hesitation. "Ain't that something? No more Nicky Nap...and so soon after Mark got iced for ratting him out to the cops."

"Mark was *never* a rat." I'm out of patience. "He never informed on Nicky or *anyone*."

"Hey, I'm on your side, I'm just saying…"

Maybe I shouldn't hang up on her, but I do. Maybe she's my bestie, maybe she's well-intentioned, but I'm *sick to death* of people thinking they *know* when they *don't*...especially *now*, after *everything*.

Don't try to tell me what you think you understand if *you* weren't the one who found Mark *dead* in the fucking *driveway*.

Don't *ever* fucking *pretend* you have a *clue* about *love*.

THE ZOMBIE RIDESHARE

I buckle in and try to cool off as we drive onward, winding through the streets of the city. There isn't much else I can do, still locked in the back of the car as I am.

Where exactly we're going, I don't know, but the zombie has me curious when he drives up onto the big Fort Pitt bridge over the Monongahela River. Why the hell, after shooting up a dead bar on the North Side for no apparent reason, would he drive out of downtown and head for the suburban South Hills?

Raul's on a similar wavelength. "Where the fuck are we going?" Maybe he noticed something different in the sound of the car when it rolled onto the bridge.

"Hold on, I'll ask Mr. Personality." I rap my knuckles on the divider. "Hey up there! Where the fuck are we going?"

As usual, the driver doesn't say a word.

"He said something about a big rock-candy mountain," I tell Raul. "Either that or the road to Shambala."

"Thanks for clearing that up. Here I thought we were on the highway to Hell."

"Close." Suddenly, we zip into a long,

brightly-lit tube with an arched ceiling. "We're in the Fort Pitt Tunnels now."

"Tell that guy he fucking sucks," says Raul. "I need for him to know that."

"I don't think he gives a shit what we think. Honestly, I don't even know if he thinks at all."

"I wonder why," says Raul. "I mean, what *is* his deal, anyway? *Is* it dementia? Maybe some kind of brain damage, like a stroke or something?"

I frown. "I don't think so. A stroke would've fucked him up worse than just putting him in a trance or whatever."

"Makes sense, I guess," says Raul. "He didn't have any trouble tying me up, throwing me in the trunk, locking you in the back, or firing the .38, did he? Not to mention driving my car like a pro."

"Then what else could it be?" I stare at the back of the driver's head, wracking my brain... then do what I should have done to begin with and start searching the 'net.

Why can someone drive but not talk, with eyes rolled up in sockets?

Just as I finish entering my search, I notice the car accelerating. We fly from the tunnel at a high rate of speed, bolting out onto the open Parkway heading south.

"What's going on?" shouts Raul.

THE ZOMBIE RIDESHARE

Looking out the back window, I spot two black Cadillac Escalades racing toward us. Both have tinted windows, so I can't see who's inside... but one has a vanity plate up front that I know all too well.

FNKBNS1

That's Frankie Beans' ride, so I know who's coming after us. Frankie doesn't let anyone but Frankie drive that motherfucking black Escalade with the special plate.

As soon as the southbound Parkway splits into more than two lanes, the Escalades leap up and flank the Camry on either side, boxing us in.

I know they're here for me—to put me down or take me in for retribution. I'm also sure they tracked my phone to find me; they've got some badass IT guys on staff with the skills to do just that. The only question is, did Ange tip them off to my current situation and give them my number, which I recently changed for security purposes? My bestie would never do something like that, now, would she?

Yes, she damn well might, if smooth-talking

Frankie somehow convinced her she'd be saving my life.

"Tell me what's going on!" hollers Raul. "Sounds like we're doing about a *hundred*."

"A pair of Escalades are chasing us down the Parkway," I tell him. "One on either side."

"Oh, great! The guy in the *coma* is gonna outrun and outmaneuver two *Escalades?*"

"The coma's gotten us *this* far, hasn't it?"

As if in reply, the driver guns the engine, and the Camry darts out ahead of the Escalades.

"What now?" asks Raul.

"We're ahead of them. This guy drives better than most people who *aren't* in a coma, if you ask me."

Just as I say that, our driver swerves violently left. The Escalade in the passing lane dodges toward the medial barrier, out of control.

Our driver wastes no time going after the other vehicle. He spins the wheel hard to the right, then chucks it left, swooping into and out of the far-right lane. Frankie's personal Escalade bucks right and falls away, but not for long. As I watch, the black SUV surges up and cuts left, coming in hard.

I brace myself for impact by seizing the grab handle on the ceiling above the passenger side

THE ZOMBIE RIDESHARE

door...but I don't need it. The zombie guns it again, bolting us out of the collision zone just in time to avoid the hit.

After that, he swoops into the far right lane, aiming for the Green Tree exit ramp. I quickly see why, as the Escalade we lost earlier hurtles toward us from behind, hell-bent on bumping us off the road.

The zombie blasts onto the ramp, then slams on the brakes and spins out of it at the last second. We barely get clear as the Escalade charges past, unable to escape the ramp and race after us.

As we roar back onto the Parkway, I hear Raul thumping around in the trunk, propelled by the series of radical maneuvers.

"Would you please *tell* him to try not to *kill* me back here?" he howls.

Just then, my phone starts ringing again—but the ringtone's generic this time, not *Wonder Woman*. Whoever's on the line, talking to them won't do me any good...but I pick it up anyway, curious.

And quickly wish I hadn't.

"*Bitch!*" Frankie Beans screams over the roar in the Escalade's cabin. "You murdered Nicky Nap, you fucking *bitch!*"

Nothing I say will make the situation better,

so I keep my mouth shut. I don't tell him how Nicky would've killed me first if I'd given him the chance. I don't tell him how *I* would've killed *Nicky* sooner if I'd known about the hit he'd ordered on Mark before it went down. I don't even tell him what a worthless sack of *shit* he is for never standing up to Nicky and now chasing down payback for his death instead of singing Hallelujah for being out from under the prick.

"Did you *hear* me, Vanessa?" Frankie's still howling on the phone like it'll somehow put the fear of God in me. "Crossin' the *line* like that, you got no way *out*. You're gonna end up *dead* like your traitor *fiancé*, and *no one's* gonna shed a fuckin' *tear* for you!"

Oh, how I wish I was driving the Camry right now, especially since that asshole's Escalade's dead ahead. We lost it when we jumped off at Greentree and hopped back on, but now we're about to catch up.

And the way the zombie's driving, I do believe he means to do the scumbag harm.

Sure enough, our driver floors it, shooting like a guided missile toward the rear of the Escalade.

Seeing the impact coming, I shout at Raul to hold on, though I doubt there's much he can do. I barely manage to brace *myself*.

THE ZOMBIE RIDESHARE

WHOOOOM

The Camry might be smaller and less powerful, but it still sends the Escalade careening left. It bounces off the medial barrier, though, and leaps back across the lanes toward our car.

"You're dead, bitch!" Frankie screams over the phone. "This is for *Nicky Nap*!"

I hang up as the Escalade skims the passenger side of the Camry, shunting us right. Unrattled as ever, the zombie steers into the slide, then cranks the wheel and stomps the accelerator at just the right second to hurl us left again.

On our way across the lanes, we clip the Escalade's nose, flinging it toward the medial once more. As we continue to sail southward, I watch through the back window as Frankie's ride crumples against the barrier and stays there. The high-speed chase down the Parkway is over, and we're free to continue onward unhindered.

With our pursuers left in the distance, a state of relative calm settles over the car. My situation still sucks, but at least I have a chance to catch my breath.

Also a chance to cut the connection that enabled Frankie and the boys to find me.

My phone has got to go. I hate to think about doing without it, but I'm also sure it's what those assholes used to pick up my trail. Even if Ange tipped them off, there's no way they could have tracked me without the phone.

Since the child locks apply to the car's rear windows as well as the doors, I can't just toss the phone onto the Parkway. I guess I'll have to stomp the hell out of it instead and hope that's enough to neutralize the tracker.

Before I go to work on it, though, I remember the Google search I set in motion before the car chase. *Why can someone drive but not talk, with eyes rolled up in sockets?*

Opening the web browser, I see the search results and scroll through them. As I do, I want to smack myself in the head, because I totally missed an obvious answer until now.

Just then, the *Wonder Woman* ringtone plays again. My grip on the phone tightens with the anger I feel toward Ange for betraying me like she did.

I know I shouldn't pick it up. I can't trust her. What I *should* do is stick to my plan and smash the phone.

Instead, I thumb the red button on the screen to take the call.

"Vaness?" she says. "Are you all right?"

No thanks to you, bitch, is what I want to tell her...but instead, I say nothing. Let her fill in the blanks on her own.

She waits, then clears her throat and continues. "I've got good news," she tells me, as if anything could possibly make this better. "I know who your *guy* is."

Again, I stay silent.

"Your driver," says Ange. "I ran an image search of a screen capture from the video you sent, and I found him. I *found* him."

Finally, I let a word slip out. "Who?"

"His name is Ernest Crandall," says Ange. "And get this: he's a *convicted murderer.*"

She lets that sink in, or maybe she expects a reaction...but she doesn't get one. As interested as I am, I won't give her the satisfaction.

"He went to prison thirty years ago for killing his wife, Linda. He insisted he was innocent, and they never found her body." She pauses again for what seems like dramatic effect. "Guess when he finally got out for good behavior and terminal illness?"

"When?"

"Two weeks ago," says Ange. "Went to stay with a family member. Guess where?"

It doesn't take a genius to see where this is heading. "Nicky Nap's neighborhood."

"Bingo."

"Well, fuck me." So this whole mess is all down to bad luck then—*my* bad luck for clipping Nicky Nap the same night a killer ex-con couch-surfing in the 'hood lost his shit and carjacked my escape ride.

"So now you know who he is, anyway," says Ange. "I can't find anything about him having a *zombie*-like condition, though. There's no mention of a stroke or dementia or..."

"He's sleepwalking," I tell her. *Also sleep-carjacking, sleep-driving, sleep-shooting, and sleep-everything-elsing.*

"Shit," says Ange. "You think so?"

"He *acts* like he's asleep," I tell her. "And he doesn't seem to be otherwise fucked up, given all the shit he can do."

"Okay, maybe," Ange says thoughtfully. "Assuming you're right, now you just have to wake his ass up without making things worse. Got any ideas?"

"I'll take care of it."

She pauses. "Vaness, hey, I'm sorry. I swear to

God, I thought I was doing the right..."

I hang up before she can finish. *She* doesn't *get* to apologize after what she did. *That* ship has *sailed*.

Now, it's down to me and Ernest.

"I know who you are, asshole," I tell him, for no good reason. It's not like he's paying attention to anything other than the nightmare playing in his head. "I know what you did to Linda."

As always, his eyes in the rearview mirror remain half-rolled-up in their sockets, betraying no sign of comprehension.

"I guess we have something in common," I tell him. "I'll bet you don't even know how alike we are."

"What the *flying fuck* are you *talking* about up there?" asks Raul, who's been quiet for a while.

I lean right, directing my voice through the gap between the backrests. "I think maybe I finally understand what's going on."

"With Ernie the wife killer, you mean? I heard bits and pieces of your phone call just now, but not all of it."

"I think he's reliving the night of the murder. He's sleepwalking through it."

"Are you *sure* he's not a fucking *zombie* in a

trance?"

As I talk, I switch off my phone and drop it on the floor. "When he shot the .38 outside Huey's... maybe that was where he killed her. Maybe, in his dream, he was blowing her away like he did the first time."

"I guess we should count ourselves lucky he didn't shoot one of *us* to make it more *real*."

"The night is still young."

"What do you mean by that? Is there something you're not telling me?"

"I'm just saying we don't know what comes next. We don't know where he's taking us."

"Well, the good news is, I finally got myself free back here," says Raul. "And I think I can jimmy the trunk release with this knife of yours. It would be easier if I could actually *see* a little, though. Can you push your phone through so I can use the flashlight?"

"No can do." I raise my right foot and bring the heel down as hard as I can on the phone, smashing the glass screen. "Damn thing just ran out of charge."

"I guess I'll have to do it by touch, then." He sounds disappointed.

"Guess so." I stomp the phone harder than before. "Murphy's Law strikes again."

THE ZOMBIE RIDESHARE

We drive for a while on the Parkway, then take Rt. 22 toward the Pittsburgh International Airport. Ernie skips the Airport exits and picks up 30 instead, zooming further from civilization into the night.

At this point, I find myself wishing I hadn't smashed my phone. Maybe I could have found some clues to our destination by researching Ernie's story. At least I don't have to worry about Frankie and the guys tracking the phone and running us down with a team of reinforcements.

And I *do* have a handful of clues, after a night of utter cluelessness. I know a *little* about who Ernie is and what he did…enough, maybe, to survive being trapped in his sleep-driving nightmare.

"Doesn't sound like much traffic out there," pipes up Raul. "Are we out in the boonies somewhere?"

Looking around, I see only trees on either side of the road and not a single car in sight. "Yep, that's about right."

"Mad killer drives his victims into the middle of nowhere," says Raul. "How many times have I heard *this* story before?"

"At least you've popped the latch on the trunk

and can fight back when we finally get where we're going, right?"

"No promises. I mean, I *almost* have it, but I don't want to risk popping it open while we're going 70 or whatever on the highway."

"Just please get me out of here when we do stop," I tell him. "Get out and get a door open so I can make a break for it."

"I'll do the best I can." Something in his voice changes unexpectedly...softens, though I can still hear him clearly through the gap cut by the stiletto. "I wanna do right by you, Vanessa. I don't know what you did tonight, the reason you ordered a getaway from Crimeshare...and I don't care. Something tell me you're still good people, y'know?"

Well, *that* was a surprise. Now, how do I tell him he just isn't my type? And by *type*, I mean *Mark*, the only person I'll ever love in this life.

Better, I think, to brush aside what Raul just said in favor of the news I now have to report. "You aren't gonna believe where Ernie is taking us," I tell him, reading a big green locator sign as we roll past it. "When you left the house tonight, did you think you'd be heading for a place called Raccoon Creek State Park?"

THE ZOMBIE RIDESHARE

How did I not notice Ernie had a shovel up there?

I finally see it when he pulls over, turns off the engine, and reaches across the cabin to pluck the tool from the floor. It's a short-handled spade, not even three feet long. He takes it with him when he gets out and shuts the door, leaving the car's headlights engaged.

What he plans to do here, I still don't know. We're deep in Raccoon Creek State Park, at the ass-end of a rutted access road with nothing around but trees and brush.

It's the perfect spot, in other words, to kill a couple of captives and plant them where they're unlikely ever to be found.

"What's he doing?" asks Raul, who's banging around as he works on the trunk latch.

"Walking up ahead of the car with a shovel." I watch as Ernie marches robotically into the bright spot cast by the headlights. "And now he's stopping."

"*Shovel?* He has a fucking *shovel?*"

"Yes, and he's digging with it." I can't look away as Ernie sinks the tip in the dirt, then drives it deeper with a foot on the upper edge of the blade.

"Digging our *graves*, I'll bet," snaps Raul. "He'll toss us right in after he blows us away with the .38."

"I don't know." The motion of the shovel is hypnotic as Ernie drives it in, scoops out loosened earth, and tosses it aside. "Where would that fit in his nightmare?"

"You mean the one about the murder of his wife? Gee, let me think." Raul bangs something hard against the metal framework of the trunk. "Could it be he's going to *kill* us like he murdered *her*?"

"Then why didn't he do it already? If he was acting out the murder back at Huey's, why didn't he shoot *us* instead of firing into thin air?"

"Gee, *I* don't know. Maybe because he's *fucked in the head?*"

"Or maybe we're just along for the ride. I mean, what if, on some level, he *wants* someone to see all this? What if we're here not as *victims* but as *witnesses?*"

"*Fuck!*" Raul goes into a frenzy of thumping movement in the back...then finally settles. "I thought I *had* this thing. I thought I could *pop* it, but it's *stuck* for some reason."

"You'll get it," I tell him. "Our luck's been so shitty, it *has* to improve."

Even as I say it, the first drops of rain patter on the car's roof. Before long, they're hammering the Camry in a full-blown downpour that even the canopy of evergreens does little to weaken or deflect.

Soon enough, Ernie is digging mud instead of dry clods of dirt. He's soaking wet, but he doesn't let it slow him down. He doesn't alter his machinelike motion, doesn't change the angle of attack or the way he throws the waste.

He's a man on a mission, whatever that mission might be.

Ernie is up to his shoulders in the hole by the time Raul finally opens the trunk.

I hear it fly up behind me before I hear his shout of victory...and my heart pounds hard with anticipation.

The next thing I know, Raul is standing outside the rear driver side door, waving in at me. It's the first time I've actually seen him, and he's older than I thought—in his forties, at least, with gray mingled with black in his curly hair and neatly trimmed chin beard. He's short, beefy, and already thoroughly soaked, his blue plaid flannel shirt and jeans plastered to his skin.

I can't help grinning as he opens the door and waves me out. I don't even care that it's pouring down rain; I'm so happy to escape, I hop out of the car without hesitation.

He reaches for a handshake, and I accept. "Great to finally meet you *face to face*," he says.

"Likewise." The smile on my face is genuine. This guy just helped me get through a real ordeal, and I'm grateful.

"By the way, I broke your knife popping the trunk latch," he says. "Sorry about that."

"No worries. Maybe Crimeshare will reimburse me for the damaged property."

"I'll get right on that. Remind me to file a claim." He laughs.

"I'll hold you to that." In spite of everything, I laugh, too.

The novelty of freedom quickly wears off as both of us turn our attention to the man in the hole.

"Now, we need the car keys." I peer in the front driver side window, looking for the keys on the steering column. "Of course he couldn't make it easy and leave them in the ignition."

"So tell me," says Raul. "This guy can sleep-drive, sleep-shoot, and sleep-dig pretty good. You think he can sleep-*fight*, too?"

"He's got a shovel and a gun, so I doubt he's a pushover."

"Yeah, but we've got the odds in our favor. It's a two-against-one situation."

"But Ernie's a convicted murderer." I look around at the dark, dense woods that extend in all directions around us. "Damn. If he hadn't driven us so far out here, we could just walk away and be done with it."

Suddenly, a flash of lightning illuminates our surroundings, forcing me to shut my eyes against the brightness. A rumble of thunder follows, echoing through the park.

When it all dies down, I notice a change in the air. Something's missing.

It doesn't take long to figure out what it is. "Listen." I point toward the hole.

"Holy shit," says Raul. "The bastard stopped digging."

Gazing into the glow cast by the headlights, I see no sign of Ernie or his shovel. If he's there—and where else could he be?—he must have dropped out of sight for some reason.

"Maybe the fucker fell and hit his head on a rock or something," says Raul.

"Or maybe he just finally fell asleep." I walk past him toward the hole. "Or maybe he finally woke up."

Raul tries to get me to stay back, but I won't. Whatever's happening in the hole, I need to see.

I just have to hope that what I see isn't the barrel of the .38 pointing up at me.

As I draw closer to the edge, I hear a new sound through the rushing of the raindrops... though I'm not sure it's what I think it is until I peer down into the hole.

When I get my first clear look, I realize Ernie's sobbing down there. He's on his knees, his body shaking with a succession of heavy, gulping sobs. His gaze is fixed on something clutched in his mud-caked hands—but it's nothing I might have expected like the shovel or gun.

It's a piece of filthy material, a hunk of cloth coated with brown muck.

"What the fuck?" Raul draws up beside me. "So he *was* diggin' for something?"

"The rest of his nightmare, I think." Watching Ernie sob, I feel a strange flicker of sympathy in my chest.

"He's still asleep?" asks Raul...and then he raises his voice for Ernie's benefit. "You still *asleep*, you old *fuck*?"

Ernie just keeps sobbing, which I think is our answer.

"Now's our chance." Raul hunkers down. "Let's kick his ass while he's out of it, grab the keys and gun, and get the fuck outta here."

It's as good a plan as any...but I hesitate. The sight of Ernie down there reminds me of myself, clutching Mark's blood-soaked shirt when I found him dead outside our apartment. The sound of his sobs reminds me of my own that night and every night since.

The truth is, I've been sleepwalking through what's left of my life, too. I've been stuck in a nightmare myself, unable to wake up. Even now, after killing Mark's killer, I don't feel like I'm free of it.

"Hey, come on," says Raul. "Let's do this before he snaps out of it."

"Stay here," I tell him. "I'll take care of this."

"Wait, no!" He grabs my arm. "Don't be stupid!"

I wave him off and lower myself into the hole.

Ernie doesn't even look at me as I drop down to kneel beside him in the muck. He just keeps sobbing and kneading that hunk of material in his gnarled hands.

From down here, I see that there's more of it in the ground. Brushing some of the mud from it, I make out a pattern—pale pink flowers over yellow, or as close to those colors as printed cloth can remain after being buried for decades.

Is the material part of a blouse or dress? Is this, then, where he buried his wife so long ago? Has he come back to mourn her, to regret what he did?

Or does he not even know in that dream of his? Is he so far gone that nothing matters anymore?

That, I can understand. I can identify.

Kneeling here with him, I'm lost, too. The reasons Mark was taken from me are as senseless as whatever inspired Ernie to kill Linda.

So what if Nicky Nap was obsessed with protecting his number two spot atop the Napolitano crime family food chain? So what if he got it in his head that golden boy Mark was destined for the top role ahead of him? So what if their dying father had always seemed to love and trust Mark more than Nicky and had hinted around about making Mark boss when he passed?

So what if Mark wanted none of Nicky's power, wanted only to be with me...but Nicky was too insecure to accept that? So what if Nicky recruited their younger brother and fellow Mark-hater, Carlo, to help ensure a *permanent solution?*

All that matters now is that Mark isn't here, and neither is Ernie's wife. Full fucking stop.

Boiled down to that, Ernie and I are two of a kind.

"What the actual *fuck?*" shouts Raul. "Am I gonna have to come down there and do it *myself?*"

Sifting through the mud, I find something else among the ruined clothing. My fingers catch on a thin chain, and I pull, bringing up the buried item from its resting place.

Lightning flashes, and I see the object for what it is—a small gold cross attached to a gold chain. The driving rain rinses it clean before my eyes, even as a bolt of thunder crashes around us.

BAWHOOOOM

Ernie sees the pendant and is transfixed.

"This was hers, wasn't it?" I dangle it before him. "Linda was wearing this when she died, wasn't she?"

With a sudden grab, he snatches it from me. Falling back against the muddy wall of the hole, he presses the cross to his cheek and sobs more violently than before.

Again, I think of Mark...remember the days

leading up to his death. Those days after he proposed marriage and I accepted were the happiest of my life, and he said they were the happiest of his, as well. I remember us walking together, hand in hand. I remember us eating and dancing and laughing and talking. I remember us making love.

I remember all the reasons I treasured every minute we spent together...and all the times I had a peek at the darkness ahead but refused to see it.

The naked hatred in his brother Nicky's face. The adoration that radiated from his father every time he and Mark were together...adoration that never showed when Nicky or Carlo were present. The bad news about his father's condition that kept getting worse, guaranteeing he had only months left to live.

I should've seen it coming.

Is that really why I feel like Ernie? Because I believe, deep down, that Mark's death is my fault? Because I, of all people, should have noticed the warning signs and didn't?

Suddenly, Raul drops into the hole and shoves his way between us. "Enough pissing around."

Ernie doesn't resist as Raul jams his hand in his pants pocket and fishes out the keys to his car. The old man's too busy staring at Linda's necklace and sobbing.

It's a different story when Raul goes for the gun, though. At first, Ernie remains docile as Raul reaches around behind him to where the .38 is stowed under his waistband.

As Raul pulls the gun out, though, Ernie's expression changes. His eyes slide down so they're no longer half-rolled-up, and his face shifts from grieving to furious. It's as if he has finally snapped out of his sleepwalking state.

With the necklace still tangled in his fingers, Ernie grabs for the .38 with both hands. The move takes Raul by surprise, and he struggles to hang on to the weapon.

Lightning flashes, and thunder booms. The rain pounds harder than ever.

There isn't much room to maneuver in the hole, but I do what I can, pounding on Ernie's arms with both fists. When that does no good, I rake his face with my nails...but he clamps his eyes shut against the clawing and continues to hold tight to the gun.

Drawing back a fist, I punch him in the throat. With a sharp gasp, he lets go of the .38 with one hand and lashes out in retaliation, flinging me hard against the muddy wall of the hole. Then, he attacks Raul's grip on the pistol with fresh fury.

"Fucking *let go!*" howls Raul.

Realizing he might just lose the battle, I quickly scan the hole for a weapon...and spy the shovel half-sunk in the muck nearby. I lunge for it, wrapping my fingers around the mud-covered handle.

Ernie roars with rage and plows Raul back into the mud with such jarring force that the gun falls free from both their grips. It splashes into the murky water in the bottom of the hole—and Ernie is the first to scramble after it.

As he plunges his hands into the muck, I know all will be lost if he comes up with the weapon. His violent instincts have taken over, turning the man who was lost in a trance of remorse into one for whom more murders are no doubt a viable path to survival.

Raising the shovel, I know I have no choice. Ernie straightens, gun in hand.

BAWHOOOOM

Screaming over a fresh bomb of thunder, I plunge the blade of the shovel into his neck and drive it as deep as my strength and momentum allow. The strike pins him to the wall as blood sprays out of the wound, mixing with the onrushing downpour.

Ernie flails at first, the .38 swinging wildly in his hand...and then he lets go of it and slumps.

"Fuck!" Raul's out of breath from the fight. "Thanks for the save!"

I'm breathing hard, too, and dazed. "Are you all right?"

"Yeah, now that *this* asshole's fucking dead!" Raul pushes himself to his feet, then hauls off and kicks Ernie hard in the belly. "Why'd he have to go and wake up *before* we got the *gun*?"

Maybe he made peace with his wife's memory? Ended the nightmare by freeing her from this unknown burial site? Or maybe I'm giving him too much credit.

"Who knows?" Bracing myself against the wall, I get up, too. "Who cares?"

Raul leans down and fishes the .38 from the deepening rainwater. "All I know is, I'm getting out of the fucking rideshare business after this. A straight-up life of crime would be *safer*, I think."

"Well, if I had to get carjacked in a rideshare tonight, I'm glad it was yours." I can't manage more than a small smile, but I turn it his way. "Thanks for getting me through this."

Raul smirks and shrugs. "Does that mean you'll give me a good rating in the app?"

"Five stars all the way."

"On that note, I say let's get the fuck out of here." Raul clambers out of the hole, then stands at the edge for a moment. "You coming?"

I nod. "Just give me a minute."

"Seriously?" He looks at me like I'm nuts. "Why?"

It's none of his business. "One minute won't kill you."

"One minute is all you get," he tells me. "It's been a long fucking night."

Then he walks away, leaving me with Ernie. I hear the car's engine start, and I see the headlights brighten.

My Crimeshare ride awaits—but things have changed. My original plan for what to do after Nicky's death—zip across town to kill Carlo—is shot to shit. It's been so many hours since I killed Nicky, I'm sure Carlo and everyone else is in the know and on the warpath...and it wouldn't take a leap of logic to figure I had something to do with it. My grief and rage over Mark's death have not been secret, and I've stupidly said some shit that might have given people the right idea about my murderous intentions.

It also wouldn't surprise me, as careful as I tried to be in foiling Nicky's home security setup, if some hidden camera in his townhouse or a neighbor's doorbell video feed caught me leaving his place after the murder. Not being a trained hit-person and lacking criminal experience in covering my tracks, I don't think it would take much to connect the dots and identify me. Hauling me in or rubbing me out would be a piece of cake for motivated individuals with access to the right resources.

Given all that, killing Carlo is off my to-do list, at least for now. So is being anywhere visible where any Napolitano or cop might get their hands on me.

I need to go on the run after this; I need to go off the grid. Change my life and try to move on, whatever it takes.

Most of all, I need to try not to end up like Ernie, trapped in a nightmare of regret. Try not to go down in a hole like him and stay there forever.

Somehow, I need to wake the fuck up before it's too late, because I'm sure that's what Mark would want me to do.

Raul hits the horn. He's done waiting.

Tears mingling with the rain, I boost myself up out of the hole and stumble through the glare of the headlights toward the car.

BE SOMEONE

ANNIE REED

The last time Gibby sat in a room like this, he'd been fifteen years old. Handcuffed to a ring welded to the plain metal table, no shoes, no wallet, no phone. Scared and angry and missing his twin.

And stupid. He'd been so stupid back then, but he hadn't known it.

The cops sitting across the table from him now probably thought he was stupid. Chained to that ring again just like back then when just a few hours ago he'd still had his freedom. That was okay. Let them think that, he didn't care. He knew better.

He felt like drumming his fingers on the cold, scarred metal tabletop. Keeping time to the song running through his head. What he really felt like doing getting the hell out of this room and jumping in a car—any old car. Stepping on the gas and just fucking leaving everything and everybody behind.

Well, almost everybody.

That was the point, wasn't it?

"Want to tell us what the hell was up with all that?" the older cop said.

He was probably a detective. Old and as rumpled as his cheap suit, nicotine stains on the insides of the first two fingers of his right hand.

Little pucker wrinkles around the edge of his mouth that came from decades of wrapping his liver-colored lips around a cigarette and sucking down smoke. The old guy reeked of it. Gibby wondered how the cop sitting next to the old fart could stand the stench.

Gibby had boosted cars from smokers before. Couldn't wait to turn those things over to the old man so he could take them to a chop shop. Disembowel those stinky pieces of trash for parts.

Disembowel. That was a good word. A ten-dollar word.

He hadn't used words like that when he'd been fifteen, but he was a whole ten years older now. He'd even gone to college. Okay, so it was community college where they had to let anybody in who had a GED, but still. He'd paid attention. Learned stuff, even some stuff nobody wanted students who partook of higher education to figure out.

Partook, that was maybe a five-dollar word. Not as pricey as disembowel.

Had Charlie ever known words like that? Maybe. Charlie had never been much for words. Gadgets and gizmos, those had been Charlie's thing.

Speed had been Gibby's.

The old cop was staring at him with tired eyes, waiting for Gibby to say something.

He didn't.

"We caught you red-handed," the other cop said.

This second cop was younger—still old compared to Gibby, but most cops were—and better put together. No rumples in that charcoal gray suit and diamond-patterned tie. His baby-blue shirt looked like it had come right out of the package. If Gibby looked hard enough, he was sure he could see fold marks and maybe a pinprick in the point of the collar where a tiny straight pin had held that point sharp in the package.

Did shirts still come that way? Had they ever, or had that just been the old man's explanation for why he only got Gibby and Charlie shirts from the Goodwill. So they wouldn't stab their fingers getting pins out of the collars.

The old man had been a bastard. Gibby wouldn't have put it past him to concoct a lie like that just to fuck with his kids.

Concoct. That was another five-dollar word, at least.

Gibby sat still, staring blankly at the two cops. They must be detectives, given the suits. Street cops wore uniforms. Street cops didn't interrogate suspects. Not that there'd be an interrogation. They could ask all the questions they wanted. Gibby didn't plan on saying anything. He was good at keeping his mouth shut.

The hard part was keeping his fingers still. Not bouncing his leg.

Not bolting off the hard metal chair that was digging into his ass and making a run for it just to see how strong the bolt on the table was really was. If the weld anchoring it in place was strong or had weakened with age. He'd popped welds before. Not with his bare hands, but hey, there was always a first time.

The second cop smelled like grilled onions and hamburger grease. Gibby would miss cheeseburgers. Not just any cheeseburger, but the ones he could get at the little stand next to where he'd been living with Nat for the last six months. Those things practically oozed grease and melted pepper jack cheese.

Small potatoes, as she would say. You figure out what you're willing to give up and what you're not, then you deal accordingly.

She'd always known he'd be willing to give her up. Her, and cheeseburgers, and even getting behind the wheel of a fast car and just letting go.

There was only one thing in the whole damn world Gibby hadn't been able to give up.

That was the whole reason he was here, after all. That one thing.

All it would cost him was the rest of his life.

The asshole had left the key in his car, almost like he was begging someone to steal it.

Nice set of wheels. Sleek and shiny and the steel gray color of the gun Gibby's brother kept hidden beneath his mattress. If their old man ever found that gun, he'd beat the crap out of both of them. Gibby's brother for stealing the gun and then keeping it for himself, and Gibby for not telling he knew the gun was there. Then the old man would sell it on the street and pocket the money.

Not that the old man would find it now. Charlie had brought it along with them tonight.

Tonight, Charlie said, they were leaving. Going to California where they could be someone. They just had to boost a good set of wheels first, not some clunker that would die as soon as they hit the interstate.

Gibby thought they were already someone.

They were Gibby and Charlie, two halves of a whole. Charlie got the smart half. And Gibby? What did he get?

"Speed, my man," Gibby always said whenever anybody asked why he wasn't as smart as his brother. "I got the speed."

Speed when he was walking. Speed when he was drumming his fingers to some song he heard playing on a loop in his head. And most especially speed when he was driving.

He was good at driving. Good at boosting cars too. Not too shabby for a fifteen-year-old kid whose old man beat the living daylights out of him if he and Charlie didn't boost at least one car every week so the old man could sell it at the chop shop. Pain was a good motivator.

Charlie said he didn't think the old man was really their father, just somebody their mom had shacked up with before she got sick and drifted away.

"Real dads don't beat their kids," Charlie said. "Real dads don't have them steal shit for them, you know?"

Gibby didn't. His sole experience with fathers was the old man, and he guessed that wasn't such a great example.

The asshole with the sleek car wasn't such a

great example either. He'd parked his car in the lot in front of a convenience store and left it unlocked with the key inside. Probably just stopping for a six-pack or something, thought he'd pop in real fast. Or maybe he was drunk already and forgot the key. Not that it mattered.

Gibby and Charlie, speed and the brains. They could boost any car they saw, old as shit or hot off the showroom floor. Gibby hotwired the oldies. And Charlie? He'd cobbled together a gizmo that could trick any car's alarm system, no matter how sophisticated, into thinking everything was hunky-dory. Said he got the idea on the internet, then fiddled with it to make it better.

Gibby didn't know how the gizmo worked, only that it did.

Charlie said that's why the old man kept them around. He said the old man sent them out to boost cars because they were minors and nothing really bad would happen to them if they got caught. The old man, if he got caught, he'd end up in prison. The only stealing he did was small-time stuff. Picking pockets or rolling drunks so wasted they'd never be able to ID him.

Family business, the old man called it. "We ain't no different than them rich folks in their mansions, stealing ordinary folks like us blind and laughing while they count their money."

Gibby didn't know any rich people so he couldn't say for sure that's what they did. The old man probably didn't know either. Most of the people he stole from were just ordinary folks like them.

Charlie had plans, though. He wanted to get away from the old man, and he figured his smarts would be the way to do it.

"The only difference between me and those computer geniuses in California is opportunity," he always said. "We get the opportunity, we're gone."

The asshole's sleek car was going to give them the opportunity.

Gibby slid behind the wheel. Charlie did his magic with the gizmo, then Gibby started the engine, turned on the headlights, and drove the car out of the parking lot.

No one came running out of the store yelling after them. No one tried to stop them. No one even seemed to notice.

"Sweet!" Charlie said, laughing.

He held out his hand, and Gibby high-fived him. Easy peasy, just how they liked it.

The old man had taught Gibby how to drive.

He'd only been twelve then, but he'd been big for his age just like Charlie. He fit just fine behind the wheel. His feet even reached the pedals without having to scoot the seat way up.

"Don't you be afraid none," the old man had said. "Only pussies are afraid behind the wheel."

Gibby had never been afraid of driving. He'd been exhilarated, a ten-dollar word he hadn't known back then. All that power thrumming through the steering wheel into his fingers. It was like the car was a part of him. Only it was a part of him that could go faster than he could ever run. When he was driving, he could go faster than the kids who had bikes could ride them, even going downhill. Gibby thought if he could go fast enough in the right kind of car, he might even be able to fly.

The asshole's sleek car was one of the nicest Gibby had ever stolen. Rich, soft seats without a single crack or scratch in the smooth leather. Not a single congealed spill around the cup holder or stray leaf or bit of road grime on the carpet in the footwell. No cigarette butts in the ashtray. It even smelled nice. Fresh. New.

Gibby didn't know the make or model and he didn't much care. He'd never gotten attached because he could never keep any of the cars he boosted. This one, he thought he could get attached to. Especially if he drove it all the way to California.

He wrapped his fingers around the thick, padded steering wheel. "You know how to get where we're going?" he asked Charlie.

He'd never driven on the interstate. He kept a map in his head of all the places where they'd boosted cars so they'd know never to go back to the same place again, and he knew how to get to the places where the old man had told them to leave the cars. But he'd never driven out of the state. Hell, he'd never been outside the city.

"West," Charlie said. "Just find a sign for the interstate and head west."

Gibby wasn't good on his east/west directions. He drove by landmarks. Onramp signs were a kind of landmark. He just had to find one that said west.

Charlie's gizmo let out a little chirping beep. "You're driving too fast," he said. "Slow down."

Gibby glanced at the speedometer. This car drove so smooth that he hadn't realized he'd been speeding. *Keep to the speed limit* had been one of the old man's rules. Use turn signals. Stop at stop signs. Don't run red lights. Don't give the cops a reason to pull you over.

He let off on the gas and glanced in the rearview mirror. He didn't see a cop, but that didn't mean anything. Cops had low-rise lights on their cop cars now. You didn't see those things until they lit them up, and by then it was too late.

Charlie's gizmo though. That chirp meant a speed gun had clocked them.

Gibby made a turn at the next intersection. He drove down the block and turned again. He found a place to pull over next to the curb. He killed the lights but left the engine running.

Play dead.

Half a minute later, headlights turned the corner behind them. A spotlight speared the car, then a siren gave a single whoop and the red-and-blue lights on the roof of the cop car that had followed them strobed into the night.

"Shit," Gibby said. "What do we do?"

It was too late to get out of the car and run. They were both fast, but nobody could outrun a bullet. The neighborhood Gibby had stopped in looked rundown, the kind the old man trolled when he was out looking to make a score. The kind of neighborhood where the cops would shoot first and ask questions later. The old man used to take his boys along to places like this when they were younger to teach them to take care of themselves.

Well, they hadn't taken care of themselves all that well tonight.

A bullhorn squawked to life, then a no-nonsense voice told them to get out of the car with their hands up.

Gibby shared a look with Charlie.

"Do what the man says," Charlie told him.

Gibby didn't want to. He didn't want to give up this car. Didn't want the old man to beat him for getting them both caught. He wanted—*needed*—to see how fast this car could really go.

He didn't think. He just slammed the transmission into drive and gunned the engine.

The sleek car leaped forward like the fast car Gibby knew it could be. He turned on the headlights and raced down the street. Took the next corner faster than he'd ever taken a corner before. The tires squealed but the car held the road like a pro.

Charlie was yelling at him, telling him to stop, that he was only making things worse, but Gibby didn't care. He thought he'd known speed before, but that had been like walking. This car was *flying,* man, just flying.

Headlights chased him, those red-and-blue

cop car lights flashing through the night, siren wailing. It might have been Gibby's imagination, but he thought the cop car was falling behind. He wanted to glance down to see how fast they were going, but he didn't dare take his eyes off the road.

"You're going to get us killed!" Charlie screamed at him.

Gibby ignored him.

C'mon, baby. Fly. Leave all this shit behind and just fucking fly!

Charlie was jabbing at his gizmo, poking the thing like Gibby had seen bigger, tougher kids at school poke the wimpy kids they were bullying. The gizmo shrieked. To Gibby it sounded like it was dying.

Then the engine in the car died. Just fucking quit. No gas, no power, not even any headlights.

"What did you do?" Gibby turned wide eyes in Charlie's direction. "What did you *do?*"

Gibby didn't see the construction cones blocking the right-hand side of the road until it was too late. The car hit the first cone and sent it flying before it plowed into the second. Beyond the cones, a mound of dirt had been piled up, excavated from a hole where the city was replacing drainage pipes that ran beneath the street.

The car, that sleek, fast, silver missile, running

blind and still going way too fast, hit that dirt at an angle. The airbags exploded. The one in the steering wheel hit Gibby square in the face and knocked him backward into his seat. The right-side tires climbed that mound of dirt, tipping the car on its side, and then they were flying.

Flying and rolling upside down.

Gibby couldn't hold onto the wheel. It was all he could do to fold his arms across his chest. Charlie was screaming again, but this time in pain. Shrieks that nearly drowned out the metallic crunches and squeals of the car's death rattle.

When the car finally came to a stop, Gibby's brains were so scrambled that when he reached for the door handle, it seemed like his arm was a million miles long and he couldn't control it. He tried to paw at the door but his body wasn't working right. Charlie was still screaming. Gibby turned his head slowly, like in a dream. They were both hanging upside down, the seatbelts holding them in place. Charlie had blood running down the side of his face, and Gibby thought he could see a bone poking out of his brother's arm.

The sight made him sick. His scrambled brains made him sick. He tried to say his brother's name, but nothing came out.

The world started to fade away.

By the time the cop who'd been chasing them made it to the wreck, gun drawn, flashlight aimed at the interior, Gibby had passed out.

Gibby didn't wake up until he was in the hospital with his ankle handcuffed to his bed's railing. Doctors came in and checked him out while two uniformed officers watched. As soon as the doctors pronounced him fit except for some bruises and minor lacerations, the cops took him to an interrogation room at the police station.

Nobody would tell him what happened to Charlie. Not the doctors at the hospital or the cops who interviewed him. Not even the court-appointed minor's advocate, a middle-aged woman with sad eyes who told Gibby to keep his mouth shut if he didn't want to go to prison.

Gibby did what he was told. He kept his mouth shut, even when the old man came to see him. The old man screamed at Gibby, told him he was a fuckup. Worthless pieces of shit, him and his brother, and that he was washing his hands of the both of them.

That was the first confirmation Gibby got that his brother had survived the crash.

After that, Gibby was transferred to a juvenile detention facility. He thought Charlie might end up in the same facility, but no dice.

Gibby was housed in that facility until he was eighteen, when he was told he'd be released and his record sealed.

On the day of his release, he expected to be reunited with Charlie. They both turned eighteen on the same day after all. But the only one waiting for him was his new advocate.

"Be a good boy," his advocate told him.

The woman he'd met in the hospital emergency room had resigned, this new guy said. She'd been sad and tired, but at least she'd seemed like she cared about Gibby. This new guy acted like he could give a shit.

When Gibby asked where his brother was, the advocate looked at his watch. "He'll be here in about…oh…fifteen or twenty years."

Gibby's mouth fell open. "We were both minors," he said.

"*You* were a joy-riding minor. Your brother was in possession of a firearm during the commission of a felony. That car was worth a lot of money. Somebody had to pay, and that was your brother. They tried him as an adult."

Gibby knew what that meant.

BE SOMEONE

The old man made them boost cars so he wouldn't go to prison. Charlie had only taken the gun because the two of them were going to California to get away from that bastard. The old man was the one who should have paid.

"Where is he?" Gibby asked. "Where did they send my brother?"

The advocate shrugged. "Don't know, don't care."

Gibby glared at him. "Aren't you a piece of shit."

The advocate sighed. He was just like the guards and the counsellors inside. Just putting in their time until they retired or found something—anything—better to do for a living.

"Look," the advocate said. "You're not a kid anymore. My duty to you ended the minute you walked out of this detention facility. Technically I don't even have to be here."

Like the guy was doing Gibby some big favor.

He felt his fingers curling into a fist. He wanted to smack this smug sonofabitch in his smug face. He could almost hear Charlie telling him to be smart. This wasn't the guy he was really mad at.

No, he was mad at the old man.

"You wanted to be someone, right?" the advocate said. "Wasn't that what you told my predecessor? Well, congratulations. You're now officially someone. You're an adult. Keep your nose clean. Next time you mess up, you can join your brother in prison for a decade or two. Maybe they'll even put you in adjoining cells."

The advocate stood there looking at Gibby, like he was waiting for Gibby to tell him thank you or something for just showing up and giving him this little speech.

Well, screw that.

Gibby turned his back on the man and started walking down a sidewalk he'd only seen from behind bars for the last three years. His left arm ached. He hadn't broken anything in the crash according to the emergency room doctor, but his left arm hurt sometimes. Like it was reminding him of how badly he'd screwed up.

He didn't know where he was going, just away from here. He had a hundred bucks in his pocket and a list of places that were basically halfway houses for kids like him. The day was cold and the sky overcast, and the street smelled like diesel fuel and old motor oil, but it was the first taste of freedom he'd had in nearly three years.

As he walked, he started going over his options. The counsellor had laid them all out during their last session. Gibby hadn't paid a whole lot of attention. Charlie had always been the planner, but Charlie wasn't going to be around for a long time. Gibby was on his own. He was going to have to take care of himself until Charlie got out.

Okay, fine. He could do that. He'd taken care of himself inside just fine. He was big enough he didn't get bullied often, and he'd worked on making himself bigger.

He just had to keep body and soul together. Be an upstanding citizen.

That's not what he wanted to do. He wanted to get even with everyone responsible for deciding to make his brother pay for what Gibby had done.

Gibby had never deluded himself. He'd been the one driving. He'd made the decision to try and outrun the cops instead of getting out of the car like Charlie had wanted them to. He'd been the one who'd wrecked the car. But his brother had gone to prison for all of Gibby's bad decisions. That wasn't fair. Gibby should have been the one they'd punished. But they'd taken it out on his brother, that anonymous *they* who'd decided someone had to pay.

Charlie would tell him to cool his heels. Be a good brother. That once he got out, they'd go to California and start over. The dream would still be there. They could still be someone. A few years wouldn't make all that much difference.

Gibby decided to listen to that calm, rational voice. Charlie had always been the smart one.

So Gibby took out the list the counsellor had given him and found a place to stay. He went back to school. Got his GED and went on to community college. He got a series of shit jobs because that was all he could get. He met women he liked and a few of them seemed to like him back. None of those relationships ever lasted. That was fine. He was just marking time until his brother got out and they could be Gibby and Charlie again. Until they could head to California to start their real lives.

He thought Charlie might actually be proud of him. He was being a good citizen.

And he kept right on being a good citizen until he got word that his brother had been killed in prison.

Gibby started with the asshole who'd left the key in the car Gibby and Charlie had boosted. That sleek, slick, shiny steel gray car that had been parked like a fucking siren in front of the convenience store.

Gibby knew about sirens now, and not just the kind that were in cop cars. He knew all that mythology shit thanks to a class he'd taken when he'd still been trying to be an upstanding citizen. Trying to make his brother proud.

He learned a lot in college, including some practical shit. Auto repair. Electronics. HVAC. He even took some criminal justice classes, not that he ever intended to be a cop. But one thing he'd learned over the years was he needed to get to know the enemy. Learn how they got their information. What was important, what wasn't. Learn their haunts and habits and the rules they operated by. Their predilections.

Predilections. That was a ten-dollar word for sure.

He found out who'd owned the car he and Charlie had stolen that night. Charlie had been tried as an adult, which meant records of his case weren't sealed. Gibby bought himself a fake ID and used it to go to the courthouse and look at his brother's file. He told the file clerk that he was prelaw and trying to get a feel for whether he wanted to go into criminal defense or civil law. He even flirted with her just enough to smooth things over.

He spent hours reading transcripts of the trial. That was how he'd learned about the car owner's shady past. The man had been arrested more than once for possession. Of course, he had the money to hire a high-priced attorney and had never done a day behind bars.

Charlie's lawyer had been a public defender. Charlie never stood a chance.

Gibby read the police reports and follow up reports. One of them mentioned that they'd found blood on the carpet in the trunk. The blood didn't belong to Charlie or Gibby or the owner of the car. Charlie's lawyer had tried to argue that the car had been left unlocked in the hopes that someone would steal it and get blamed for the blood. The judge hadn't bought it.

That was when Charlie's lawyer had cut him a deal. Actually had the whole thing worked out with the prosecutor, but the judge wouldn't approve it.

"You don't get out of this that easily, young man," the judge had told Charlie. "You had a gun. A gun you admit was stolen. Someone's got to pay for what happened, and that someone is you."

The judge had sentenced Charlie to twenty years without parole.

Case closed.

Not for Gibby.

He knew now why the car had been left open with the key inside. It was just like Charlie's lawyer said. The owner just had to wait for some chump to come along and steal it, and that would be that. He'd never be arrested for whatever he'd done that had left blood all over the carpet in the trunk.

Well, the hell with that.

Gibby tracked down the man's current address. He staked out the man's house. Followed him to where he worked. Followed him to his mistress's house, where he parked his brand new sleek and shiny car—this one white, like he thought he was one of the good guys—at the curb.

While the man was inside spending time with whoever he was screwing, Gibby slid beneath the car. He could probably boost this one, take it for a spin. Set it sailing off a cliff or roll it into a lake, but that wasn't good enough. Instead he put a neat little hole in the brake line.

Two days later there was a brief item on the news. The man had died in a single-car accident when he plowed through an intersection and rammed into a concrete abutment head-on. Witnesses said the car didn't even slow down.

Someone had to pay, right? Wasn't that what the judge had said at Charlie's trial?

Gibby thought the judge was right on the money. Someone did have to pay. A bunch of someones, just not Charlie.

And Gibby was the man to make sure that happened.

Next on his list was the prosecutor who'd decided that Charlie should be tried as an adult. Gibby planted cocaine in the man's gym bag, enough to put him over the limit from possession to possession with intent to sell. He'd found out that the man had been in a detox program, a successful one by all accounts.

Or at least that's what his colleagues thought until he was arrested.

"Welcome to prison, asshole," Gibby had said when the prosecutor's arrest hit the news. "See how you like it."

Gibby wasn't stupid, not anymore. The prosecutor would probably get a plea deal, but his days as a lawyer were over. Convicted felons couldn't practice law.

Next on his list was the judge. That sanctimonious asshole who'd refused to accept Charlie's plea bargain.

Judges were supposed to be impartial. Were supposed to apply the law equally to whoever appeared in their court.

That wasn't the case with this judge. Gibby spent more time digging through court files for the cases this guy had decided in the last ten years. He eventually discovered a pattern, probably because he was the only one with the time and the determination to go looking for it.

Poor defendants got screwed in this guy's court. It didn't matter if the case was civil or criminal, if the defendant was black or white or brown. Poor defendants in criminal cases got jail time. Rich defendants got suspended sentences or their cases outright dismissed.

More digging turned up information on the judge's private life. How he hobnobbed with the rich and famous—at least the famous as far as their city went. How they took him on junkets, paid for cruises for him and his wife. All to curry favor in his court. Fellow judges who openly opposed this guy either lost their re-election bids or quietly and suddenly resigned.

Gibby revised his earlier conclusions. He probably wasn't the first one who'd researched this judge. He just had nothing left to lose, and therefore had no reason to stop. He especially didn't give a shit that the judge turned out to be a very big fish in a relatively small pond.

He'd heard that saying in the juvenile detention facility, only there the guards had turned it around. As in, "You might be hot shit in your little gang in the outside world, but in here you ain't nothing but a small fish in a very big pond that don't give a shit about you."

By the time Gibby was researching the judge, he'd moved in with Nat. She was good people. Covered most of their expenses so he could spend more time getting his plan for the judge just right.

"You're good at this stuff," she said. "You put your mind to it, you could be an investigative reporter, you know that?"

Investigative. That had to be a five-dollar word.

Gibby figured he probably could be, but that was not where he was headed.

He had a totally different end game in mind.

BE SOMEONE

The two detectives sat watching him. Detective Nicotine Stain and Detective Freshly Pressed. They looked like mismatched bookends, waiting for him to spill his guts.

Lots of cops thought silence was a good motivator. (Motivator was another five-dollar word.) That once they chained someone up and stared at them, saying nothing, the tension would make a person talk.

Gibby knew better than that. He could keep his mouth shut. He'd kept his mouth shut all those years ago, hadn't he? He shouldn't have, but he did. He certainly wasn't going to give in now.

Finally Freshly Pressed opened a folder he'd brought in with him. "Twenty-two people are in the hospital," he said. "Including the judge and his wife and the governor." He slapped the folder down on the table. "You can't tell me you didn't know what you were doing."

Gibby didn't say anything. He didn't even let himself smile.

The detectives shared a look, then Nicotine Stain looked back to Gibby.

"Your fingerprints are on the remote," he said.

"All over the equipment. What I don't get is that you made no effort to hide it was you."

Of course not. Gibby had wanted to be found.

He'd waited to put his plan into motion until the night the judge and his wife were entertaining some of the local rich and famous. Corporate bigwigs who wined and dined the judge and his wife. The governor, who'd appointed the judge to the bench in the first place and threw his considerable support behind the judge whenever he came up for re-election. Who touted the judge's tough on crime stance to the very people the judge was throwing in jail right and left.

People could be so stupid.

All Gibby'd had to do was wear a uniform. HVAC service. Annual maintenance, he'd told the maid who'd answered the door. She didn't check with anyone to make sure the visit was valid. Gibby didn't think she would. The staff had been running around like crazy, preparing the judge's multi-million dollar estate for the party.

Not that the staff would be in attendance. The judge had hired a catering company owned by one of his cronies. Gibby had made sure of that before he picked this particular night to make the judge shoulder at least some small portion of the responsibility for what happened to Charlie.

Gibby's uniform let him go about his business like he was invisible. Rich people—people who thought they were so very important—didn't notice the people who did all the menial tasks they couldn't do themselves.

Menial. Was that a five-dollar word? No. Two at the most. Gibby didn't care about two-dollar words.

He'd disabled all the carbon monoxide monitors in the mansion. Disabled all the fire alarms. Plugged the pipes that vented that pesky carbon monoxide from the three different gas furnaces located throughout the mansion into the outside air. Ran a hose from the tailpipe of the judge's very expensive car to another pipe that carried hot air from one furnace in the garage into the central part of the mansion. He'd thought about setting up a gas generator in the garage as well, but he didn't want to kill anyone. He just wanted to make them sick.

All of them.

Most especially the judge.

The last thing he did was pair a remote to the judge's car. Gibby still wasn't as good with electronics as Charlie had been, but remotes for cars had come a long way. This one would start the judge's car without Gibby being anywhere near it.

He'd thought about pocketing the remote and taking it with him, but he wanted the police to find it. So he'd left it in the driveway in front of the closed garage door. Just like a calling card.

He'd waited for the police at the fast-food joint where he worked nights. He didn't want them to find out about Nat. She'd agreed to move and leave no forwarding address, just in case. And if they found her? She'd disavow any knowledge of what he'd done.

Disavow. That was a five-dollar word for sure.

Detective Nicotine Stain must have decided not to wait Gibby out. Not to try and bully him. He sighed and leaned back in his chair.

"We ran your name through the system," he said. "Juvenile record, sealed. Your brother's isn't. You two got yourself in a serious mess, but you got out of it relatively unscathed."

Unscathed. Another five-dollar word.

"You have a hard-on for this judge, is that it?" Nicotine Stain asked. "You think this little prank was a good way to get back at him? Well, this wasn't just a prank. People got hurt. They got sick. You're going to have to pay for what you did, you understand that, don't you?"

Pay for what he did. Of course he understood that. That's what this was all about.

Not that he was going to tell the detectives that.

He leaned back in his chair, mirroring Nicotine Stain's posture. He didn't let his fingers tap out a rhythm to the song playing in his head, or bounce his leg to tap his foot on the concrete floor. He'd given them nothing so far, all according to plan.

But then he did something he hadn't planned. That he couldn't have stopped if he tried.

He smiled.

He was still smiling when they led him away and locked him in a cell.

All according to plan. He was pretty sure Charlie couldn't have come up with anything better.

It took Gibby three more years to put the finishing touches on his plan.

Three years of being a model prisoner. Of doing everything he got told to do. Of being assigned first to one facility and then moved to another facility and moved again until he was finally incarcerated as part of the general population in a prison that housed non-violent offenders.

Like twenty-something assholes who'd pulled ridiculous pranks, according to the warden.

Chop shop minions who paid for stolen cars then sold the parts for a handsome profit.

Thieves and pickpockets and drunk drivers on their third strike who'd managed not to kill anyone.

Gibby had killed someone—the owner of the car he and Charlie had boosted—but no one knew about that. One of the benefits of keeping his mouth shut.

He got a job working in the prison laundry for peanuts, and spent most of the time when he wasn't shoving sheets in an industrial dryer in his cell reading. He read a lot of books, picked up a bunch more five- and ten-dollar words along the way, and just bided his time. He was ready for what came next. He just had to pick the right moment.

That moment came when he was out in the yard, walking in circles around the perimeter—but not too close to the perimeter—when he felt someone come up next to him. He didn't have to look. He knew who it was. In fact, he was surprised it had taken the old man so long to approach him.

"Always knew you were no good," Gibby's old man said.

He was older now, they both were, but the years hadn't been kind to the old man. He'd lost a lot of weight. The flesh under his chin hung in loose wattles. His eyes had sunk in on themselves, and his nose was riddled with spider veins. He had the same nicotine stains on his fingers as that detective had when Gibby'd been arrested after he'd fucked with the judge.

Gibby wondered if wattles was a five-dollar word. He'd changed his categories somewhat thanks to all his reading. It took way more for a word to make it into the five-dollar category, much less the ten-dollar one.

Gibby didn't say anything, just turned to look at the old man.

He must have gotten slow. Gotten stupid. Must have thought he could still lift wallets and roll drunks and not get caught. Gibby had done more than just research the judge. He knew the old man was doing a solid fifteen. More than Gibby was in for, at least for now.

It seemed so stupid that Gibby had ever let this piece of shit intimidate him. Use the threat of pain to keep him in control. One punch and Gibby could have knocked the old man out. Then Charlie wouldn't have needed the gun.

Something in Gibby's eyes must have registered with the old man. His expression turned wary, like he knew there'd been a shift in their relationship. That he couldn't rely on past beatings to keep Gibby in line.

The old man held one hand up in a placating gesture. "No harm, no foul," he said. "I didn't want anything to do with you then. Don't want anything to do with you now."

Placating. That was a five-dollar word, right?

The thought made Gibby smile.

"But I want something to do with you," he said.

He didn't punch the old man. Didn't stab him. He wrapped both hands around that scrawny neck and squeezed.

Working in the laundry had made Gibby's hands strong. Both of them, even his left. His fingers were like vise grips. He pressed his thumbs against the old man's throat and felt his voice box give way.

The old man's face turned purple. Gibby kept squeezing. He was still squeezing when one of the guards ran over and hit him with a taser.

By then the old man was dead.

"What the fuck?" the guard said over and over. "What the hell was that for?"

The taser wasn't a high-powered model. Why should it be? All the prisoners here were non-violent. The cells weren't even locked until lights out at night.

Gibby lay on the hardpacked dirt of the exercise yard, looking up at the clear blue sky. Not a cloud in sight. He wouldn't be seeing the outside world for a long time, but that was okay.

Somebody had to pay, that shitass judge had told Charlie all those years ago. Somebody had to pay.

It shouldn't have been Charlie. Not Charlie. Gibby had made sure the ones who'd been responsible for what happened to Charlie had paid. The car's owner. The prosecutor. The judge and those who'd enabled him.

There'd been two other people left who still had to pay. Gibby had just killed one of them.

As for the other one?

Killing the old man the way he did, out in the open for all to see, Gibby had made sure the only other person would be paying with the rest of his life. However long that might be.

Two guards hauled Gibby to his feet. They

cuffed his hands behind his back and perp-walked him back inside the prison. Threw him in a windowless cell and slammed the door shut behind him.

No one was around this time to see him smile. Or to hear him tell his dead twin that he was finally someone.

I'm vengeance, Gibby thought. Irrefutable, irrevocable retribution.

Then he laughed.

Those were ten-dollar words, each and every one of them.

READ MORE!

Never miss an issue of Mystery, Crime, and Mayhem! Get yourself a subscription!

https://www.mysterycrimeandmayhem.com/product/mcm-subscription/

For the latest news, sign up for the newsletter here:

https://www.mysterycrimeandmayhem.com/never-miss-a-release/

In addition to learning about all the great issues, you'll also get a free copy of the *MCM Criminally Good Anthology*.

OUR FRIENDS

Friends of MCM
    Knotted Road Press
    Pub Share
    BookFunnel
    Thrill Ride The Magazine
    WMG Publishing
    Sisters in Crime
    I Found This Great Book
    Crime Writers of Color
    One House Productions

Milton Keynes UK
Ingram Content Group UK Ltd.
UKHW020131070524
442290UK00014BC/675